KEN MACLEOD

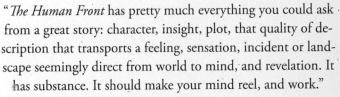

NO LONGER PROPERTY OF SEATTLE PUBLIC LIBRARY

Winner of the
Prometheus Award
BSFA Award
Sidewise Award

"*The Human Front* has pretty much everything you could ask from a great story: character, insight, plot, that quality of description that transports a feeling, sensation, incident or landscape seemingly direct from world to mind, and revelation. It has substance. It should make your mind reel, and work."
—Iain M. Banks

"As much fun as [Macleod's] books provide, it's that fierceness, that seriousness of purpose, that powers their engines and makes me want to read on."
—*Locus*

"*The Human Front* is a complete knock out . . . elegant, eloquent and laugh-out-loud funny. And that last quality by itself makes it worth the very weird trip."
—Rick Kleffel, *The Agony Column*

"Ken MacLeod brings dramatic life to some of the core issues of technology and humanity."
—Vernor Vinge

D0032136

LIBRARY OF THE
UNIVERSITY OF

PM PRESS OUTSPOKEN AUTHORS SERIES

The Human Front

plus...

The Human Front

plus

"Other Deviations: The Human Front Exposed"

and

"The Future Will Happen Here, Too"

and

"Working the Wet End"
Outspoken Interview

KEN MACLEOD

PM PRESS | 2013

Ken MacLeod © 2013
This edition © 2013 PM Press

"The Future Will Happen Here, Too" was first published November 2010 in *The Bottle Imp*, the e-zine of the Scottish Writing Exhibition, published by the Association for Scottish Literary Studies. *The Human Front* was first published as a chapbook in 2001 by PS.

Series editor: Terry Bisson

ISBN: 978-1-60486-395-6
LCCN: 2012913630

10 9 8 7 6 5 4 3 2 1

PM Press
P.O. Box 23912
Oakland, CA 94623

Printed in the USA on recycled paper by the Employee Owners of Thomson-Shore in Dexter Michigan
www.thomsonshore.com

Outsides: John Yates/Stealworks.com
Insides: Jonathan Rowland
Author photograph by Julie Howden © *The Herald*

CONTENTS

THE HUMAN FRONT

LIKE MOST PEOPLE OF my generation, I remember exactly where I was on March 17, 1963, the day Stalin died. I was in the waiting-room of my father's surgery, taking advantage of the absence of waiting patients to explore the nicotine-yellowed stacks of *Reader's Digest*s and *National Geographic*s, and to play in a desultory fashion with the gnawed plastic soldiers, broken tin tanks, legless dolls and so forth that formed a disconsolate heap, like an atrocity diorama, in one corner. My father must have been likewise taking advantage of a slack hour towards the end of the day to listen to the wireless. He opened the door so forcefully that I looked up, guiltily, though on this particular occasion I had nothing to be guilty about. His expression alarmed me further, until I realised that the mixed feelings that struggled for control of his features were not directed at me.

Except one. It was with, I now think, a full awareness of the historic significance of the moment, as well as a certain sense of loss, that he told me the news. His voice cracked slightly, in a way I had not heard before.

"The Americans," he said, "have just announced that Stalin has been shot."

"Up against a wall?" I asked, eagerly.

My father frowned at my levity and lit a cigarette.

"No," he said. "Some American soldiers surrounded his headquarters in the Caucasus mountains. After the partisans were almost wiped out they surrendered, but then Stalin made a run for it and the American soldiers shot him in the back."

I almost giggled. Things like this happened in history books and adventure stories, not in real life.

"Does that mean the war is over?" I asked.

"That's a good question, John." He looked at me with a sort of speculative respect. "The Communists will be disheartened by Stalin's death, but they'll go on fighting, I'm afraid."

At that moment there was a knock on the waiting-room door, and my father shooed me out while welcoming his patient in. The afternoon was clear and cold. I mucked about at the back of the house and then climbed up the hill behind it, sat on a boulder and watched the sky. A pair of eagles circled their eyrie on the higher hill opposite, but I didn't let that distract me. After a while my patience was rewarded by the thrilling sight of a V-formation of American bombers high above, flying east. Their circular shapes glinted silver when the sunlight caught them, and shadowed black against the blue.

• • •

The newspapers always arrived on Lewis the day after they were printed, so two days passed before the big black headline of the *Daily Express* blared STALIN SHOT, and I could read, without fully comprehending, the rejoicing of Beaverbrook, the grave commentary of Cameron, the reminiscent remarks of Churchill, and frown over Burchett's curiously disheartening reports from the front, and smile over the savage raillery of Cummings's cartoon of Stalin in hell, shaking hands with Satan while hiding a knife behind his back.

Obituaries traced his life: from the Tiflis seminary, through the railway yards and oilfields of Baku, the bandit years as Koba, the October Revolution and the Five Year plans, the Purges and the Second World War; his chance absence from the Kremlin during the atomic bombing of Moscow in Operation Dropshot, and his return in old age to the ways and vigour of his youth as a guerrilla leader, rallying Russia's remaining Reds to the protracted war against the Petrograd government; to the contested, gruesome details of his death and the final, bloody touch, the fingerprint identification of his hacked-off hands.

By then I had already had a small aftershock of the revolutionary's death myself, at school on the 18th. Hugh Macdonald, a pugnacious boy of nine or so but still in my class, came up to me in the playground and said: "I bet you're pleased, *mac a dochter*."

"Pleased about what?"

"About the Yanks killing Stalin, you *cac*."

"And why should I not be? He was just a murderer."

"He killed Germans."

Hugh looked at me to see if this produced the expected change of mind, and when it didn't he thumped me. I kicked his shin and he ran off bawling, and I got the belt for fighting.

That evening I played about with the dial of my father's wireless, and heard through a howl of atmospherics a man with a posh Sassenach accent reading out eulogies on what the Reds still called Radio Moscow.

The genius and will of Stalin, great architect of the rising world of free humanity, will live forever.

I had no idea what it meant, or how anyone even remotely sane could possibly say it, but it remained in my mind, part of the same puzzle as that unexpected punch.

• • •

My father, Dr. Malcolm Donald Matheson, was a native of the bleak long island. His parents were crofters who had worked hard and scraped by to support him in his medical studies at Glasgow in the 1930s. He had only just graduated when the Second World War broke out. He volunteered for combat duty and was immediately assigned to the Royal Army Medical Corps. Of his war service, mainly in the Far East, he said very little in my hearing. It may have been some wish to pay back something to the community which had supported him which led him to take up his far from lucrative practice in the western parish of Uig, but of sentiment towards that community he had none. He insisted on being addressed by the English form of his name, instead of as "Calum" and I and my siblings were likewise identified: John, James, Margaret,

Mary, Alexander—any careless references to Iain, Hamish, Mairead, Mairi or Alasdair met a frown or a mild rebuke. Though a fluent native speaker of Gaelic, he spoke the language only when no other communication was possible— there were, in those days, a number of elderly monoglots, and a much larger number of people who never used the English language for any purpose other than the telling of deliberate lies. There are two explanations, one fanciful and the other realistic, for the latter phenomenon. The fanciful one is that they believed that the Gaelic was the language of heaven (was the Bible not written in it?) and that the Almighty did not hear, or did not understand, the English; or, at the very least, that a lie not told in Gaelic didn't count. The realistic one is that English was the language of the state, and lying in its hearing was indeed legitimate, since the Gaels had heard so many lies from it, all in English.

My mother, Morag, was a Glaswegian of Highland extraction, who had met and married my father after the end of the Second World War and before the beginning of the Third. She, somewhat contrarily, taught herself the Gaelic and used it in all her dealings with the locals, though they always thought her dialect and her accent stuck-up and affected. The thought of her speaking a pure and correct Gaelic in a Glasgow accent is amusing; her neighbours' attitude towards her well-meant efforts less so, being an example of the characteristic Highland inferiority complex so often mistaken for class or national consciousness. The Lewis accent itself is one of the ugliest under heaven, a perpetual weary resentful whine—the Scottish equivalent of Cockney—and the dialect thickly corrupted with English words Gaelicised by the simple expedient of mispronouncing them in the aforementioned accent.

Before marriage she had been a laboratory assistant. After marriage she worked as my father's secretary, possibly for tax reasons, while raising me and my equally demanding brothers and sisters. Like my father, she was a smoker, a whisky-drinker, and an atheist. All of these were, at that time and place, considered quite inappropriate for a woman, but only the first was publicly known. Our non-attendance at any of the three doctrinally indistinguishable but mutually irreconcilable churches the parish supported was explained by the rumour—perhaps arising from my father's humanitarian contribution to the war effort—that the *dochter* was a Quaker. It was a notion he did nothing to encourage or to dispel. The locals wouldn't have recognised a Quaker if they'd found one in their porridge.

Because of my father's military service and medical connections, he had stroll-in access at the nearby NATO base. This sprawling complex of low, flat-roofed buildings, Nissen huts, and radar arrays disfigured the otherwise sublime headland after which the neighbouring village, Aird, was named. My father occasionally dropped in for cheap goods—big round tins of cigarettes, packs of American nylons for my mother, stacks of chewing-gum for the children, and endless tins of corned beef—at the NAAFI store.

It was thus that I experienced the event which became the second politically significant memory of my childhood, and the only time when my father expressed a doubt about the Western cause. He was, I should explain, a dyed-in-the-wool conservative and unionist, hostile even to the watery socialism of the Labour Party, but he would have died sooner than to vote for the Conservative and Unionist Party. "The Tories took our land," he once spat, by way of explanation, before slamming the door in the face of a rare, hopeless canvasser. He showed less emotion at Churchill's death than he did at Stalin's. So, like most of our neighbours, he was a Liberal. The Liberals had, in their wishy-washy Liberal way, decried the Clearances, and the Highlanders have loyally returned them to Parliament ever since.

Why the Highlanders nurse a grievance over the Clearances was a mystery to me at the time, and still is. In no land in the world is the disproportion between natural attraction and sentimental attachment more extreme, except possibly Poland and Palestine. Expelled from their sodden Sinai to Canada and New Zealand the dispossessed crofters flourished, and those who remained behind had at last enough land to feed themselves, but their descendants still talk as if they'd been put on cattle trucks to Irkutsk.

It was my habit, when I had nothing better to do on a Saturday, to accompany my father on his rounds. I did not, of course, attend his consultations, but I would either wait in the car or brave the collies who'd press their forepaws on my shoulders and bark in my face, to the inevitable accompaniment of cries of "Och, he's just being friendly," and make my way through mud and cow-dung to the hospitality of black tea in the black houses, and the fussing of immense mothers girt in aprons and shod in wellingtons.

We'd visited an old man in Aird that morning in the summer of '63, and my father turned the Hillman off the main road and up to the NATO base. Gannets dropped like dive-bombs in the choppy sea of the bay below the headland's cliffs, and black on the Atlantic horizon the radar turned. Though militarily significant—Lewis commands a wide sweep of the North Atlantic, and Tupolev's deep-shelter factories in the Urals were turning out long-range jet bombers at a rate of about one a month, well above attrition—security was light. A nod to the squaddie on the gate, and we were through.

My father casually pulled up in the officers' car-park outside the NAAFI and we hopped out. He was just locking the door when an alarm shrieked. Men in blue uniforms were suddenly rushing about and pointing out to sea. Other men, in white helmets and webbing, were running to greater purpose. Somewhere a fire-engine and an ambulance joined in the clamour.

I spotted the incoming bomber before my father did, maybe two miles out.

"There—there it is!"

"It's *low*—"

Barely above the sea, flashing reflected sunlight as it yawed and wobbled, trailing smoke, the bomber limped in. On the wide concrete apron in front of us a team frantically pushed and dragged a big Wessex helicopter to the perimeter, while one man stood waving what looked like outsize ping-pong bats. The bomber just cleared the top of the cliff, skimmed the grass—I could see the plants bend beneath it, though no blast of air came from it—and with a screaming scrape and a shower of sparks it hit the concrete and slithered to a halt about a hundred yards from where we stood.

It was perhaps fifty feet in diameter, ten feet thick at the hub. Smoke poured from a ragged nick in its edge.

The ambulance and fire-engine rushed up and stopped in a squeal of brakes, their crews leaping out just as a hatch opened on the bomber's upper side. More smoke puffed forth, but nothing else emerged. A couple of firemen, lugging fire-extinguishers, leapt on the sloping surface and dropped inside. Others hosed the rent in the hull.

My father ran forward, shouting "I'm a doctor!" and I ran after him. The outstretched arm of one of the men in white helmets brought my father up short. After a moment of altercation, he was allowed to go on, while I struggled against a firm but not unfriendly grip on my shoulder. The man's armband read "Military Police." At that moment I was about ten yards from the bomber, close enough to see the rivets in its steel hull.

Close enough to see the body which the firemen lifted out, and which the ambulancemen laid on a stretcher and ran with, my father close behind, into the nearest building. It was wearing a close-fitting silvery flying-suit, and a visored helmet. One leg was crooked at a bad angle. That was not what shot me through with a thrill of horror. It was the body of a child, no taller than my five-year-old sister Margaret. The large helmet made its proportions even more child-like.

A moment later I was turned around and hustled away. The military policeman almost pushed me back into the car, told me to wait there, and shut me up with a stick of chewing-gum before he hurried off. Everybody else who'd come at all close to the craft was being rounded up into a huddle guarded by the military policemen and being lectured by a couple of men who I guessed were civilians, if their snap-brimmed hats, dark glasses and black suits were anything to go by. They reminded me of American detectives in comics. I wondered excitedly if they carried guns in shoulder holsters.

After about fifteen minutes my father came out of the building and walked over to the car. One of the civilians intercepted him. They talked for a few minutes, leaning towards each other, their faces close together, one or other of them shaking their fingers, pointing and jabbing. Each of them glanced over at me several times. Although I had the side window wound down, I couldn't hear what they were saying. Eventually my father turned on his heel and stalked over to the car, while the other man stood looking after him. As my father opened the car door the black-suited civilian shook his head a little, then rejoined his colleague as the small crowd dispersed.

A knot of military policemen formed up at the building's doorway, and surrounded two stretcher-bearers as they hurried to the Wessex. There was only the briefest glimpse of the stretcher as it was passed inside, moments before it took off and headed out to sea on a southerly course.

My father's face was pale and his hand shook as he took his hip-flask from the glove compartment. The top squeaked as he unscrewed it, the flask gurgled as he drank it dry.

"Leave the window down, John," he said as he turned the key and pushed the starter. "I need a cigarette."

He lit up, fumbling, then engaged the gears and the car moved off with a lurch. As we passed the soldier on the gate my father gave him a wave that was almost a salute.

"What sort of people will that poor laddie be fighting for?" he asked me, or himself. His knuckles were white on the wheel. The swerve on to the main road threw me against the door. He didn't notice.

"Monsters," he said. "Monsters."

I sat up straight again, rubbing my shoulder.

"It's awful to use wee children to fly bombers," I said.

He looked across at me sharply, then turned his attention back to the single-track road.

"Is that what you saw?" he murmured. "Well, John, we were told very firmly that the pilot was a midget, you know, a dwarf, and that this is a secret. If the enemy knew that, they would know something they shouldn't know about our bombers. About how much weight they can carry, or something like that."

I squirmed on the plastic leather, swinging my legs as though I needed to pee. I had read about dwarfs and midgets in *Look and Learn*. They were not like in fairy stories.

"But that's not true," I said. "That wasn't a dwarf, the pro—the portions—"

"'Proportions.'"

"The proportions were wrong. I mean, they were right—they were ordinary. The pilot was a child, wasn't he?"

The car swerved slightly, then steadied.

"Listen, John," my father said. "Whatever the pilot is, neither of us is supposed to talk about it, and we'll get into big trouble if we do. So if you're sure it was a child you saw, I'm not going to argue with you. And if the Air Force say the pilot is a midget, I'm not going to argue with them, either. I set and splinted the leg of that, that"—he

hesitated, waving a hand dangerously off the wheel—
"*craitur beag 'us bochd*—of the poor wee thing, I should
say, and that's all I know of it."

I was as startled by his lapse into the Gaelic as by
the uncertainty and ambiguity of his reference to the pilot,
and I thought it wise to keep quiet about the whole sub-
ject. But he didn't, not quite yet.

"Not a word about it, to anyone," he said. "Not to
your mother, your brothers and sisters, your friends, anyone. Not a word. Promise me?"

"All right," I said. I was young enough to feel that it
was more exciting to keep a secret than to tell one.

The following day was a Sunday, and although it
meant nothing to us but a day off school we had to conform to local custom by not playing outside. It was a sweltering hell of boredom, relieved only by the breath of air
from the open back door and the arrival at the front door
of two men in black suits, who weren't ministers. My father escorted them politely into his surgery. The waiting-
room door (I found, on a cautious test) was locked. They
did not stay long; but the following morning on the way
out to catch the van to school I overheard my mother tele-
phoning around to postpone the day's appointments, and
noticed a freshly emptied whisky bottle on the trash.

• • •

A couple of years later, when I was ten, my father sold his
practice to a younger, less financially straitened and more
idealistic doctor (a Nationalist, to my father's private dis-
gust) and took up a practice in Greenock, an industrial

town on the Firth of Clyde. Our flitting was exciting, our arrival more so. It was another world. In the mid-1960s the Clyde was booming, its shipyards producing naval and civilian vessels in almost equal proportion, its harbours crowded with British and American warships, the Royal Ordnance Factory at Bishopton working around the clock. Greenock, as always, flourished from the employment opportunities upriver—beginning with the yards and docks of the adjacent town of Port Glasgow—and from its own industries, mainly the processing of colonial sugar, jute and tobacco. The pollution from the factories and refineries was light, but fumes from the heavy vehicular traffic that serviced them may well explain the high incidence of lung cancer in the area. (My father's death, though outside the purview of the present narrative, may also be so accounted.) Besides these traditional industries, a huge IBM factory had recently opened (the ceremonial ribbon cut by Sir Alan Turing himself) in the Kip Valley behind the town.

The town's division between middle class and working class was sharp. On the eastern side of Nelson Street lay the tenements and factories; to the west a classical grid of broad streets blocked out sturdy sandstone villas and semi-detached houses. Though our parents' disdain for private education saved us from the worst snobberies of fee-paying schools, the state system was just as blatantly segregated. The grammar schools filled the offices of management, and the secondary moderns manufactured workers. Class division shocked me: after growing up among the well-fed, if ill-clad, population of Lewis, I saw the poorer eight-tenths of the town as inhabited by misshapen dwarfs.

It was while exploring what to my imagination were dangerous, Dickensian slums, but which were in reality perfectly respectable working-class districts, that I first encountered evidence that this division was regarded, by some, as part of the greater division of the world. On walls, railway bridges and pavements I noticed a peculiar graffito, in the shape of an inverted "Y" with a cross-bar—a childishly simple, and therefore instantly recognisable, representation of the human form. Sometimes it was enclosed by the outline of a five-pointed star, and frequently it was accompanied by a scrawled hammer and sickle. These last two symbols were, of course, already familiar to me from the red flags of the enemy.

It was at first as shocking a sight as if some Chinese or Russian guerrilla had popped out of a manhole in the street, and it gave me a strange thrill—a *frisson*, as the French say—to find that the remote and gigantic foe had his partisans in the streets of Greenock as much as in the jungles of Malaya or the rubble of Budapest. One day in 1966 I actually met one, on a street corner in the East End, down near the town centre where the big shops began.

This soldier of the Red horde was a bandy-legged old man in a cloth cap, selling copies of a broadsheet newspaper called the *Daily Worker*. He met with neither hostility nor interest from the passers-by. With boyish bravado, and some curiosity, I bought it. Its masthead displayed the two symbols I already knew, and an article inside was illustrated by, and explained, the third.

"Against the warmongers and arms profiteers, against the reckless drive to destruction, against the forces of death, it is necessary to rally all who yearn for peace. The situation cries out for the broadest possible united front, one broader even than the great People's Fronts against fascism, one in which every decent human being, every worker, every woman, every honest businessman, every farmer, every patriot can take their place with pride and determination. It is not for any political party, or class, or ideology that such a front shall stand, but for the very survival of the human race.

"This greatest of all united and people's fronts exists, and is growing.

"It is the Human Front."

I understood barely a word of it, and the only reason why I clipped out the article and kept it, long after I had secretly disposed of the newspaper, long enough for me to reread and finally understand it, years later, was because of coincidental resonances of its author's name—Dr. John Lewis.

• • •

After that initial naive exploration I settled down to a sort of acceptance of the world as it was, and to learning more about it, at school and out. Science was more interesting than politics, and it soothed rather than disturbed the mind. The war was a permanent backdrop of news, and a distant prospect of National Service. The BBC brought it home on the wireless and, increasingly, on black-and-white television, with feigned neutrality and unacknowledged censorship. News items that raised questions about the war's conduct and its domestic repercussions were few: the Pauling trial, the Kinshasa atomic bombing, the occasional allusion to a speech by Foot in the Commons or Wedgewood-Benn in the Lords.

The biggest jolt to the consensus came in 1968, with the May Offensive. Out of nowhere, it seemed, the supposedly defeated *maquis* stormed and seized Paris, Lyons, Nantes, and scores of other French cities. Only carpet-bombing of the suburbs dislodged them and saved the Versailles government. This could not be hidden, nor the first anti-war demonstrations in the United States: clean-cut students chanting "Hey! Hey! JFK! How many kids did you kill today?" until the dogs and fire-hoses and tear-gas cleared the streets. At the time, I was more frightened by the unexpected closeness of the Communist threat than shocked by the measures taken against it.

My first act of dissidence wasn't until three years later, at the age of seventeen. I slipped out one April evening to attend a meeting in the Cooperative Hall held under the auspices of Medical Aid for Russia. The speaker was touring the country, and it may have been the controversy that followed him that drew the crowd of a hundred or so. It's certainly what drew me. He was flanked on the platform by a local trade union official, a pacifist lady, and Greenock's perennially unsuccessful Liberal candidate. (The local Labour MP had, naturally, denounced the meeting in the *Greenock Telegraph*.) The hall was bare, decorated with a few union banners and a portrait of Keir Hardie. I sat near the back, recognising no one except the little old man who'd once sold me the *Daily Worker*.

After some dull maundering from the union official, the pacifist lady stood up and introduced the speaker, the

Argentine physician Dr. Ernesto Lynch. A black-haired, bearded man, about forty, asthmatic, charismatic, apologetic about his cigar-smoking and his English, he brought the audience to their feet and sent me home in a fury.

"You're too gullible," my father said. "It's all just Communist propaganda."

"Hiroshima, Nagasaki, Moscow, Magnitogorsk, Dien Bien Phu, Belgrade, Kinshasa!" I pounded the names with my fist on my palm. "They happened! Nobody *denies* they happened!"

He lidded his eyes and looked at me through a veil of cigarette smoke. Bare elbows on the kitchen table, mother in the next room, the hiss of water on the iron, the Third Programme concerto in the background.

"If you had seen what I saw in Burma," he said mildly, "you wouldn't be so sorry about Hiroshima and Nagasaki. And the men who went into the Vorkuta camps weren't sorry about Moscow, and—"

"And what troops 'liberated' Siberia?" I raged. "The dirty Japs! With their hands still bloody from Vladivostok! Their hands *and* their—"

I stopped myself just in time.

"Look, John," he said. "We could go on shouting at each other all night about which side's atrocities are worse. The very fact that we can, that this Argentine johnny can tour the country and half the bloody Empire with his tales of heroic partisans in the Ukraine and sob stories about butchered villagers in Byelorussia, while nobody from our side could possibly do anything remotely similar in the Red territories, shows which side has the least to fear from the truth."

"Britain didn't let the Nazis speak here during the war—William Joyce was hanged—"

He poured another whisky, and offered me one. I accepted it, ungraciously.

"We listened to Lord Haw-Haw and Tokyo Rose for a *laugh*," he was saying. "Then they were decently hanged, or decently jailed."

"Pity we're on the same side now," I said. "Maybe the Yanks should let Tokyo Rose *out*. 'Ruthki soldjah, you know what ith happening to you girrfliend? Big niggah boyth ith giving her big niggah—'"

Again, I shut up just in time.

"Your racial prejudices are showing, young man," Malcolm said. "I thought Reds were supposed to be against the colour bar."

"Huh!" I snorted. "I thought Liberals were!"

"The colour bar will come down in good time," he said. "When both whites and coloureds are ready for it. Meanwhile, the Reds will be happy to agitate against it, while out of the other side of their mouths they'll spout the most blatant racialism and national prejudice, just as it suits them—anything to divide the free world."

"Some free world that includes the American South, South Africa, Spain, Japan, and the Fourth Reich! That holds on to Africa with atom bombs! That relies on the dirty work of Nazi scientists!"

He tapped a cigarette and looked at it meditatively.

"What do you mean by that?"

"The bombers. They're what's made the whole war possible, from Dropshot onwards, and it was the Germans who invented them—to finish what Hitler started!"

He lit up, and shook his head.

"Werner von Braun died a very disappointed man," he said. "Unlike the rocket scientists the Russians got. They got to see their infernal researches put to use all right, with dire consequences for our side—mostly civilian targets, I might add, since you seem so upset about bombing civilians. At least our bomber pilots risk their own lives, unlike the Russian missilemen who deal out death from hundreds of miles away."

I could see what he was doing, deflecting our moral dispute into a purely intellectual, historical debate, and I was having none of it.

"Yeah, I wonder if the Yanks are still sending *children* up to fly the bombers."

He almost choked on his sip of whisky. Through the open door of the living-room came the sound of the iron crashing to the floor and my mother's shout of annoyance. A moment later she said, sharply: "James! Margaret! Off to bed!" A faint protest, a scurry, a slam. She bustled through, hot in her pinny, and closed the door and sat down. Her flush paled in seconds. My father glanced at her and said nothing.

They both looked so frightened that I felt scared myself.

"What's—what did—?"

My mother leaned forward and spoke quietly.

"Listen, Johnny," she said. I bristled; she hadn't called me that for years. She sighed. "John. You're old enough to do daft things. You could go off and join the Army tomorrow, or you could get married, and there's not a thing we could do about either. And it's the same with listening to Communists and repeating their rubbish. It's a free country. Ruin your prospects if you like. But there's one thing I ask you. Just one thing. Don't ever, ever, *ever* say anything about what you and your father saw in Aird. Don't even drop a hint. Because if you do, you'll ruin us all."

"You never said this to me before!"

"Never thought we had to," Malcolm said gruffly. "You kept your mouth shut when you were a wee boy, as you promised, and good for you, and I thought that maybe over the years you had forgotten all about it."

"How could I forget that?" I said.

He shrugged one shoulder.

"All right, all right," I said. "But I don't understand why it's such a big secret. I mean, surely the age or is it the *size* of the—"

My father leaned across the table and put his hand across my mouth—not as a gesture, as a physical shutting up.

"Not one word," he said.

I leaned back and made wiping movements.

"OK, OK," I said. "Leave that aside. What were we talking about before? Oh yes, you were saying it wasn't the Nazis who invented the flying disc. So who do you think did?"

"Who knows? The Allies had Einstein and Oppenheimer and Turing and a lot of other very clever chaps, and it's all classified anyway, so, as I said—who knows?"

"How do you know it *wasn't* the Germans, then?"

"They weren't working along these lines."

"Oh, come on!" I said. "I've seen pictures of the things from during the war."

"These were experimental circular airframes with entirely conventional propulsion," he said. "That doesn't describe the bombers, now does it? Have you ever heard of Nazi research into anti-gravity?"

"Have you ever heard of American?"

He shook his head.

"It's all classified, of course. But it was obviously a bigger breakthrough than the atomic bomb. Consider the Manhattan Project, and all the theory that led up to it." He paused, to let this sink in. "What I'd like you to do, John, is to use your head as well as keep your mouth shut. By all means rattle off the standard lefty rant about Nazi scientists, but do bear in mind that you're talking nonsense."

I was baffled. My mother was looking worried.

"But," I said, "the *Americans* say it was German scientists who developed it."

"They do indeed, John, they do indeed."

He looked quite jovial; I think he was a little bit drunk.

"I think you've said enough," my mother told him.

"That I have," he said. "Or too much. And you too, John. You have homework to do tonight and school to go to tomorrow. Goodnight."

• • •

The following day I felt rather flat, whether as a result of the unaccustomed glass of whisky or my father's successful deflection of my moral outrage. After school I walked straight to the public library. My parents never worried if I didn't come home from school directly, so long as I phoned if I wasn't going to be home for my tea. The library was a big Georgian-style pile in the town centre. I stepped in and breathed the exhilarating smell of dark polished wood and of old and new paper. It took me only a minute to Dewey-decimal my way around the high stacks to the aviation section. Sheer nostalgia made me reach for the first in the row of tiny, well-worn editions of the *Observer's Book of Aircraft*. I still had that 1960 edition, somewhere at home. Flicking past the familiar silhouettes of Lancaster and Lincoln and MiG, I looked again at the simplest outline of the lot: the circular plan and lenticular profile of the Advanced High Altitude Bomber, Mark 1. The description and specifications were understandably sparse ("outperforms all other aircraft, Allied and enemy") the history routine: first successful test flight, from White Sands to Roswell Army Air Field, New Mexico, July 1947; first combat use, Operation Dropshot, September 1949; extensive use in all theatres since.

I replaced the volume and pulled out the fresh 1970 edition, its cover colour photo of a Brabant still glossy. The AHAB's description, specs, and history were identical, and identically uninformative, but the designation had changed. Checking back a couple of volumes, I found that the AHAB-2 had come into service in 1964.

It didn't take me much longer to find that the biggest military innovation of the previous year had been the Russian MiG-24, capable of reaching a much higher altitude than its predecessors. I sought traces of the AHAB in more detailed works, one of which stated that none had ever been shot down over enemy territory.

All of that got me thinking, but what struck me even more was that after more than twenty years there wasn't a dicky-bird about the machine's development, beyond the obviously (now that it was pointed out) misleading references to wartime German experimental aircraft. Nor were there any civilian or wider military applications of the revolutionary physical principles behind its anti-gravity engine.

I tried looking up anti-gravity, in other stacks: physics, military history, biography. Beyond the obvious fact that it was used in the AHAB, there was nothing. No speculation. No theory. No big names. No obscure names. Nothing. Fuck all.

I walked home with a heavy load of books and a head full of anti-gravity.

• • •

"Outer space," said Ian Boyd, confidently. Four or five of us were sitting out a free period on our blazers on damp grass on the slope of the hill above the playing-field. Below us the fourth-year girls were playing hockey. Now and again a run or swerve would lift the skirt of one of them above her knees. We were here for these moments, and for the more reliable sight of their breasts pushing out their crisp white shirts.

"What d'ye mean, outer space?" asked Daniel Orr.

"Where they came frae. The flying discs."

"Oh aye. Dan Dare stuff."

"Don't you Dan Dare me, Dan Orr."

This variant on a then-popular catch-phrase had us all laughing.

"We know there's life out there," Ian persisted. "Astronomers say there's at least lichens on Mars, they can see the vegetation spreading up frae the equator every year. An it's no that far-fetched there's life on Venus an a', underneath the cloud cover."

"No evidence of intelligent life, though," Daniel said.

"No up there," said Colin McNicol. "There is down there."

"Aye, there's life, but is it intelligent?"

We all laughed and concentrated for a while on the hockey-playing aliens, with their strange bodies and high-pitched cries.

"It's intelligent," said Ian. "The problem is, how dae we communicate?"

"No, the *first* problem is, how do we let them know we're friendly?"

"Tell them we come in peace."

"And we want to come inside."

"*If*," I said, mercilessly mimicking our Classics teacher, "you gentlemen are quite ready to return the conversation to serious matters—"

"This is serious a' right!"

"Future ae the entire human race!"

"Patience, gentlemen, patience. Withhold your ejaculations. Your curiosity on these questions will be soon be fully satisfied. The annual lecture on 'Human Reproduction In One Minute' will be prematurely presented to the boys later this year by Mr. Hughes, in his class on Anatomy, Physiology, and Stealth. The girls will simultaneously and separately receive a lecture on 'Human Reproduction In Nine Months' as part of their Domestic Science course. Boys and girls are not allowed to compare notes until after marriage, or pregnancy, whichever comes sooner. Meanwhile, I understand that Professor Boyd here has a point to make."

"Oh aye, well, if it wisni the Yanks an' it wisni the Jerries, it must hae come frae somewhere else—"

"The annual prize for Logic—"

"—so it must hae been the Martians."

"—has just been spectacularly lost at the last moment by Professor Boyd, after a serious objection from Brother William of Ockham—"

"Hey, nae papes in our school!"

"—who presents him, instead, with the conical paper cap inscribed in memory of Duns Scotus, for the *non sequitur* of the year."

• • •

Near the High School was a park with a couple of reservoirs. Around the lower of them ran a rough path, and its circumambulation was a customary means of working off the stodge of school dinner. A day or two after our frivolous conversation, I was doing this unaccompanied when I heard a hurrying step behind me, and turned to see Dan Orr catch me up. He was a slim, dark, intense youth who, though a month or two younger than me, had always seemed more mature. The growth of his limbs, unlike mine, had remained proportionate, and their movements under the control of the motor centres of his brain. His father was, I believe, an engineer at the Thompson yard.

"Hi, Matheson."

"Greetings, Orr."

"Whit ye were saying the other day."

"About the bombers?"

"Naw." He waved a hand. "That's no an issue. We'll never find out, anyway, and between you an me I couldni give a flying fuck if they were invented by Hitler himsel, or the Mekon of Mekonta fir that matter."

"That's a point of view, I suppose." We laughed. "So what is the issue?"

"Come on, Matheson, ye know fine well whit the issue is. It isnae where they *came* frae. It's where they *go*, and whit they *dae* to folk."

"Aye," I said cautiously.

"Ye were at that meeting, right?"

"How would you know if I was?"

"Yir face is as red as yir hair, ya big teuchter. But not as red as Willie Scott of the AEU, who was on the platform and gave a very full account o the whole thing tae his Party branch."

"Good God!" I looked sideways at him, genuinely astonished. "You're in the CP?"

"No," he said. "The Human Front."

"Well kept secret," I said.

He laughed. "It's no a secret. I just keep my mouth shut at school for the sake o the old man."

"Does he know about it?"

"Oh, aye, sure. He's Labour, but kindae a left-winger. Anyway, Matheson, what did you think about what Dr. Lynch had tae say?"

I told him.

"Well, fine," he said. "The question is, d'ye want tae dae something about it?"

"I've already put my name down to raise money for Medical Aid."

"That's good," he said. "But it's no enough."

We negotiated an awkward corner of the path, leaping a crumbled culvert. Orr ended up ahead of me.

"Dr. Lynch," he said over his shoulder, "had some other things tae say, about what people can do. And we're discussing them tonight." He named a cafe. "Back room, eight sharp. Drop by if ye like. Up tae you."

He ran on, leaving me to think.

●●●

Heaven knows what Orr was thinking of, inviting me to that meeting. The only hypothesis which makes sense is that he had shrewdly observed me over the years of our acquaintance, and knew me to be reliable. I need not describe the discussion here. Suffice it to say that it was in response to a document written by Lin Piao which Dr. Lynch had clandestinely distributed during his tour, and which was later published in full as an appendix to various trial records. I was not aware of that at the time, and the actual matters discussed were of a quite elementary, and almost entirely legal, character, quite in keeping with the broad nature of the Front. It was only later that

I was introduced to the harsher regimens in Dr. Lynch's prescription.

We started small. Over the next few weeks, what time I could spare from studying for my Highers, in evenings, early mornings, and weekends, was taken up with covering the town's East End and most of Port Glasgow with the slogans and symbols of the Front, as well as some creative interpretations of our own.

FREE DUBCEK, we wrote on the walls of the Port Glasgow Municipal Cleansing works, in solidarity with a then-famous Czechoslovak guerrilla leader being held incommunicado by NATO. To the best of my knowledge it is still there, though time has worn the "B" to a "P."

And, our greatest coup, on the enormous wall of the Thompson yard, in blazing white letters and tenacious paint that no amount of scrubbing could entirely erase:

FORGET KING BILLY AND THE POPE

UNCLE JOE'S OUR ONLY HOPE

The Saturday after the last of my Higher exams, I happened to be in the car with my father, returning from a predictably disastrous Morton match at Cappielow, when we passed that slogan. He laughed.

"I must say I agree with the first line," he said. "The second line, well, it takes me back. Good old Uncle Joe, eh? I must admit I left 'Joe for King' on a few shit-house walls myself. Amazing that people still have faith in the old butcher."

"But is it really?" I said. I told him of my long-ago (it seemed—seven years, my god!) playground scrap over the memory of Stalin.

"It's fair enough that he killed Germans," Malcolm said. "Or even that he killed Americans. The problem some people, you know, have with Stalin is that he killed *Russians*, in large numbers."

"It was a necessary measure to prevent a counter-revolution," I said stiffly.

Malcolm guffawed. "Is that what they're teaching you these days? Well, well. What would have happened in the SU in the '30s if there had been a counterrevolution?"

"It would have been an absolute bloody massacre," I said hotly. "Especially of the Communists, and let's face it, they were the most energetic and educated people at the time. They'd have been slaughtered."

"Damn right," said Malcolm. "So we'd expect—oh, let me see, most of the Red Army's generals shot? Entire cohorts of the Central Committee and the Politburo wiped out? Countless thousands of Communists killed, hundreds of thousands sent to concentration camps, along with millions of ordinary citizens? Honest and competent socialist managers and engineers and planners driven from their posts? The economy thrown into chaos by the turncoats and time-servers who replaced them? A brutal labour code imposed on the factory workers? Peasants rack-rented mercilessly? A warm handshake for Hitler? Vast tracts of the country abandoned to the fascist hordes? That the sort of thing you have in mind? That's what a counterrevolution would have been like, yes?"

"Something like that," I said.

"That's exactly what happened, you dunderheid! Every last bit of it! Under Stalin!"

"How do we know that's not just propaganda from our side?"

"Here we go again," he sighed. "It's like arguing with a Free Presbyterian minister."

"Come on," I said. "We know that a lot of what we're told in the press is lies. Look at the rubbish they were writing about how France was pacified, right up until the May Offensive! Look at—"

"Yes, yes," he said. He pulled the car to a halt in the comfortable avenue where we lived, up by the golf course. He leaned back in his seat, took off his driving gloves and lit a cigarette.

"Look, John, let's not take this argument inside. It upsets your mother."

"All right," I said.

"You were saying about the press. Yes, it's quite true that a lot of lies are told about the war. I'll readily admit that, however much I still think the war is just. It was the same in the war with Hitler. Only to be expected. Censorship, misguided patriotism, wishful thinking—truth is the first casualty, and all that. So tell me this—who, in this country, has done the most to expose these lies?"

"Russell, I guess," I said. After that I could only think of exiles and refugees from the ravaged Continent. "And there's Sartre, and Camus, and Deutscher—"

"That's the man," he said. "Deutscher. Staunch Marxist. Former Communist. Respected alike by the *Daily Worker* and the *Daily Telegraph*. Man of the Left, man of integrity, right?"

"Yes," I said, suspecting that he was setting me up for another fall. He was. When we went inside he handed me a worn volume from his study's bowed bookshelves.

Deutscher's *Stalin*, published in 1948, was a complete eye-opener to me. I had never before encountered criticism of Stalin or his regime from the Left, nor so measured a judgement and matchless a style. It seemed to come from a vanished world, the world before Dropshot, before the Fall.

•••

"Fuck that," said Dan Orr. "Deutscher's a Trotskyite, for all that he's all right on the war. And Trotskyites are *scum*. I don't give a fuck how many o them Stalin killed. He didnae kill *enough*. There were still some alive tae be ministers in the Petrograd puppet government, alang wi all the Nazis and Ukrainian nationalists and NTS trash that the Yanks scraped out o the camps where they belonged."

I didn't have an answer to that, at the time, so I shelved the matter. In any case we had more urgent decisions to make. Although we had not had our results yet, we both knew we had done well in our Highers, and could have gone straight to University the following September. This would have deferred our National Service until after graduation. Graduates could sign up for officer training. Most of our similarly successful classmates rejoiced at the opportunity to avoid the worst of the hardships and risks. Orr was adamant that we should not take it. It was a principle with him (and with the Front, and with the Young Communist League of which, unknown to me at the time, he was a clandestine member).

"It's a blatant class privilege," he said. "Every working-class laddie has tae go as soon as he turns eighteen.

Why should we be allowed tae dodge the column for four mair years? What gies us the right tae a cushy number? And think about it—when we've done our stint that'll be it over, we can get on wi university wi none o that growing worry about what's at the end o it, and in the meantime we'll hae learned to use a rifle and we can look every young worker in the eye, because we'll hae been through the same shit as he has."

"But," I said, "suppose we find ourselves shooting at the freedom fighters?"

Or shot by them, was what was really worrying me.

"Cannae be helped," said Orr. He laughed. "I'm told it seldom comes tae that anyway. It's no like in the comics."

My mother objected, my father took a more fatalistic approach. There was a scene, but I got my way.

We spent the summer working to earn some spending money and hopefully put some by in our National Savings Accounts. In the permanent war economy it was easy enough to walk into a job. Orr, ironically enough, became a hospital porter for a couple of months, while I became a general labourer in the Thompson yard. We joked that we were working for each other's fathers.

The shipyard astounded me, in its gargantuan scale, its danger and din, and its peculiar combination of urgent pace and trivial delay. The unions were strong, management was complacent, work practices were restrictive and work processes were primitive. Parts of it looked like an Arab *souk*, with scores of men tapping copper pipes and sheets with little hammers over braziers. My accent had me marked instantly as a teuchter, a Highlander, which though humiliating was at least better than being written off as middle class. The older men had difficulty understanding me—I thought at first that this was an accent or language problem, and tried to conform to the Clydeside usage to ridiculous effect, until I realised that they were in fact partially deaf and I took to shouting in Standard English, like an ignorant tourist.

The Party branch at the yard must have known I was in the Front, but made no effort to approach me: I think there was a policy, at the time, of keeping students and workers out of each other's way. This backfired rather because it enabled me to encounter my first real live Trotskyist, who rather disappointingly was a second-year student working there for the summer. We had a lot of arguments. I have nothing more to say about that.

Most days after work I'd catch the bus to Nelson Street, slog up through the West End to our house, have a bath and sleep for half an hour before a late tea. If I had any energy left I would go out, ostensibly for a pint or two but more usually for activity for the Front. The next stage in its escalating campaign, after having begun to make its presence both felt and overestimated, was to discourage collaboration. This included all forms of fraternisation with American service personnel.

Port Glasgow is to the east of Greenock, Gourock to the west. The latter town combines a douce middle-class residential area and a louche seafront playground. Its biggest dance-hall, the Cragburn, a landmark piece of '30s architecture with a famously spring-loaded dance floor, draws people from miles around.

Orr and I met in the Ashton Cafe one Friday night in July. Best suits, Brylcreemed hair, scarves in our pockets. Hip-flask swig and gasper puff on the way along the front. The Firth was in one of its Mediterranean moments, gay-spotted with yachts and dinghies, grey-speckled with warships. Pound notes at the door. A popular beat combo, then a swing band.

We chose our target carefully, and followed her at distance after the dance. Long black hair down her back. She kissed her American sailor goodbye at the pier, waved to him as the liberty-boat pulled away. We caught up with her at a dark stretch of Shore Street, in the vinegar smell of chip-shops. Scarves over our noses and mouths, my hand over her mouth. Bundled her into an alley, up against the wall. We didn't need the masks, not really. She couldn't look away from Orr's open razor.

"Listen, slag," he said. "Youse are no tae go out wi anybody but yir ain folk frae now on. Get it? Otherwise we'll cut ye."

Tears glittered on her thick mascara. She attempted a nod.

"Something tae remind ye," Orr said. "And tae explain tae yir friends."

He clutched her hair and cut it off with the razor, as close to the scalp as he could get. He threw the glistening hank at her feet and we ran before she could get out her first sob.

I threw up on the way home.

Three days later I overheard two lassies at the busstop. They were discussing the incident, or one like it. There had been several such, over the weekend, all the work of the Front.

"Looks like you're in deid trouble fae now on," one of them concluded, "if ye go out wi coons."

• • •

Call-up papers arrived in August, an unwelcome 18th-birthday present. After nine weeks' basic training I was sent to Northern Ireland, where I spent the rest of my two-year stint guarding barracks, munitions dumps and coastal installations. Belfast, Londonderry, south Armagh: the most peaceful and friendly parts of the British Empire.

Orr was sent to Rhodesia. His grave is in the Imperial War Cemetery in Salisbury.

I was demobilised in September 1974, and went to Glasgow University. My fellow first-year students were all two years younger than me, including those in the Front. The Party line had changed. Young men were being urged to resist the war, to refuse conscription, to take any deferral available, to burn their call-up papers if necessary, to fill the jails. This was not because the Party had become pacifist. It was because the Party, and the Front, now had enough men with military experience for the next step up Lin Piao's ladder.

People's War.

• • •

It is necessary to understand the situation at the time. By 1974 the United States, Britain and the white Dominions, Germany, Spain, Portugal and Belgium were almost the only countries in the world without a raging guerrilla war.

Although nominally on the Allied side, the governments of France and Italy were paralysed, large tracts of both countries ungovernable or already governed by the Resistance movements. Every colony had its armed independence movement, and every former socialist country had its reliberated territory and provisional government, even if driven literally underground by round-the-clock bombing.

"The peoples of the anti-imperialist camp long for peace every day," wrote Lin Piao. "Why do the peoples of the imperialist camp not long for peace? Unfortunately it is because they have no idea of what horrors are being suffered by the majority of the peoples of the world. It is necessary to bring the real state of affairs sharply to their attention. In order for the masses to irresistibly demand that the troops be brought home, it is necessary for the people's vanguard to bring home the war."

• • •

That later came to be called the Lin Piao "Left" Deviation. At the time it was called the line. I swallowed it whole.

I lodged in a bed-sitting-room in Glasgow, near the University, and took my laundry home at weekends. During my National Service I had only been able to visit occasionally, and had followed the Front's advice to keep my head down and my mouth shut about politics, on duty or off. It was a habit that I found agreeable, and I kept it. My parents assumed that my National Service had knocked all that nonsense out of me.

Greenock had changed. The younger and tougher and more numerous successors of the likes of Orr and I had shifted their attacks from the sailors' girlfriends to the sailors, and the soldiers. They never attacked British servicemen, or even the police. At least a dozen Americans had been fatally stabbed, and two shot. Relations between the Americans and the town's population, hitherto friendly, had become characterised by suspicion on one side and resentment on the other. The cycle was self-reinforcing. Before long Americans were being attacked in quite non-political brawls, and off-duty Marines were picking fights with surly teenagers. The teenagers' angry parents would seek revenge. Other relatives would be drawn in. Before long an American serviceman couldn't be sure that any sweet-looking lass or little old lady wasn't an enemy.

Armed shore patrols in jeeps became a much more common sight. In the tougher areas, kids would throw stones at them. None of this was covered in the national press, and the *Greenock Telegraph* buried such accounts in brief reports of the proceedings of the Sheriff Court, but the *Daily Worker* reported similar events around U.S. bases right across Britain.

I did not get involved in them. The first petrol-bombing, in January 1975, happened when I was in Glasgow. The first return fire from a group of U.S. naval officers trapped in a stalled and surrounded staff car on the coast road—they'd started going further afield, to the quieter, smaller resort of Largs—took place in February, also midweek, when I was definitely not in Greenock. I read a brief report of it in the *Glasgow Herald*.

What was going on in Glasgow was political stuff, anti-war agitation, leafleting and picketing, that sort of thing. We took a hundred people from Glasgow to the big autumn demo in London. A hundred thousand or so converged on Grosvenor Square, with a militant contingent of ten thousand people chanting "We shall fight! We shall win!" (we all agreed on that) and the Front's hotheads following it up with "Joe! Joe! Joe Sta-lin!" or "Long live Chairman Lin!" and the Trots trying to drown us out with a roar of "London! Paris! Rome! Berlin!"

It was fun. I was serious. I knuckled down to the study of chemistry and physics (at Glasgow they still called the latter "Natural Philosophy") which had always fascinated me. The Officer Training Corps would have been a risky proposition for me—even my very limited public political activity would have exposed me to endless hassles and security checks —but I joined the university's rifle club, which shared a shooting range and an armoury with the OTC. And I was still, of course, in the Reserves. Following the Front's advice, I kept out of trouble and bided my time.

• • •

I had seen the diagram a hundred times, and its physical manifestation, the iron filings forming furry field-lines on a sheet of paper with a magnet under it, in my first-year physics class at High School. I had balanced magnets on top of each other, my fingers preventing them from flicking around and clicking together, and had felt the uncanny invisible spring pushing them apart. It was late one night in February 1975 when I was alone in my room, propping my head over an open physics textbook, that I first connected that sensation with my childhood chance observation of the curiously unstable motion of an anti-gravity bomber close to the ground, and with the magnetic field lines.

Was it possible, I wondered, that anti-gravity was a polar opposite of gravity, that keeping it stable was like balancing two magnets one upon the other, and that the field generated by the ship had the same shape as that of a magnet? If so, any missile approaching an AHAB bomber from above or below would be deflected, whereas one directed precisely at its edge, where the two poles of the field balanced, might well get through. The crippled bomber I'd seen had taken a hit edge-on, if that distant memory was reliable. The chance of that happening accidentally, even in a long war, might be slim enough for to have happened only once. Yet the consequences of doing it deliberately were so awesome that this very possibility might well be the secret which the dark-suited security men had been so anxious to maintain. It seemed much more significant than the minor, if grim, detail that the pilots were children or dwarfs.

It was an interesting thought, and I considered whether it might be possible to pass it upwards through the Front and thence across to the revolutionary air forces. Come to think of it, to pass on all I knew, and all I'd seen at Aird. The thought made me shiver. I could not get away from the idea, so firmly instilled by my parents, that anything I might say along those lines would be traced back to me, and to them.

The Allied states, and Britain in particular, had at the time a sharp discontinuity in tolerance—their liberal and democratic self-definition almost forced them to put up with radical opposition, and to treat violent opposition as civil disorder rather treason; while at the same time the necessities of the long war inclined them to totalitarian methods of maintaining military and state secrecy. A Front supporter could preach defeatism openly, and would receive at the worst police harassment and mob violence. A spy, or anyone under suspicion of materially aiding the enemy, would disappear and never be heard of again, or be summarily tried and executed. Rumours of torture cells and concentration camps proliferated. To what extent these were true was hard to judge, but irrelevant to their effect.

So I kept my theory to myself, and sought confirmation or refutation of it in war memoirs. Most from the Red side were stilted and turgid. Those from former Allied soldiers were usually better written, even if sensationalised. If these accounts were reliable at all, the AHAB bombers were occasionally used for close air support and even medevac, in situations where (as my careful cross-checking made clear) there was little actual fighting in the vicinity and the weather was too violent for helicopters or other conventional aircraft.

I put my ideas about that on the back burner and got on with my work, until the Front had work for me. I left my studies without regret. It was like another call-up, and another calling.

● ● ●

Davey stopped screaming when the morphine jab kicked in. Blood was still soaking from his trouser-leg all over the back seat of the stolen getaway car. He'd taken a high-velocity bullet just below the knee. Whatever was holding his shin on, it wasn't bone. In the yellow back-street sodium light all our faces looked sick and strange, but his was white. He sprawled, head and trunk in the rear footwell, legs on the back seat. I crouched beside him, holding the tourniquet, only slowing down the blood loss.

Andy, in the driver's seat, looked back over his shoulder.

"Take him tae the hospital?"

It was just up the road—we were parked, engine idling, in a back lane by the sugarhouse. The molasses smell was heavy, the fog damp and smoky.

"We could dump him and run," Gordon added pointedly, looking out and not looking back.

Save his leg and maybe his life for prison or an internment camp. No chance. But the Front's clandestine field hospitals were already overloaded tonight—we knew that from the news on the car radio alone.

"West End," I said. "Top of South Street."

Andy slid the car into gear and we slewed the corner, drove up past the hospital and the West Station and around the roundabout at a legal speed that had me seething, even though I knew it was necessary. No Army patrols in this part of town, but there was no point in getting pulled by the cops for a traffic offence.

We stopped in a dark spot around the corner from my parents' house. Andy drove off to dump the car and Gordon and I lugged Davey through a door in a wall, past the backs of a couple of gardens, over a fence and into the back porch. I still had the keys. It had been two years since I'd last used them.

Balaclava off, rifle left behind the doorway, into the kitchen, light on. Somebody was already moving upstairs. I heard the sound of a shotgun breech closing.

"Malcolm!" I shouted, past the living-room door. "It's just me!"

He made some soothing sounds, then said something firmer, and padded downstairs and appeared in the living-room doorway, still knotting his dressing-gown. His face looked drawn in pencil, all grey lines. Charcoal shadows under the eyes. He started towards me.

"You're hurt!"

"It's not my blood," I said.

His mouth thinned. "I see," he said. "Bring him in. Kitchen floor."

Gordon and I laid Davey out on the tiles, under the single fluorescent tube. The venetian blind in the window was already closed. My father reappeared, with his black bag. He washed his hands at the sink, stepped aside.

"Kettle," he said.

I filled it and switched it on. He was scissoring the trouser-leg.

"Jesus Christ," he said. "Get this man to a hospital. I'm not a surgeon."

"No can do," I said. "Do what you can."

"I can stop him going into shock, and I can clean up and bandage." He looked up at me. "Top left cupboard. Saline bag, tube, needle."

I held the saline drip while he inserted the needle. The kettle boiled. He sterilised a scalpel and forceps, tore open a bag of sterile swabs, and got to work quickly. After about five minutes he had Davey's wound cleaned and bandaged, the damaged leg splinted and both legs up on cushions on the floor. A dose of straight heroin topped up the morphine.

"Right," Malcolm said. "He'll live. If you want to save the leg, he must get to surgery right away."

He glared at us. "Don't you bastards have field hospitals?"

"Overloaded," I said.

His nose wrinkled. "Busy night, huh?"

Davey was coming to.

"Take me in," he said. "I'll no talk."

My father looked down at him.

"You'll talk," he said; then, after a deep breath that pained him somehow: "But I won't. I'll take him to the Royal, swear I saw him caught in crossfire." He looked out at the rifles in the back porch, and frowned at me. "Any powder on him?"

I shook my head, miserably.

"We didn't even get a shot in ourselves."

"Too bad," he said dryly. "Right, you come with me, and you, mister," he told Gordon, "get yourself and your guns out of here before I see you, or them."

Gordon glanced at me. I nodded.

"Through the cemetery," I said.

I only just remembered to remove the revolver from Davey's jacket pocket. My mother suddenly appeared, gave me a tearful but silent hug, and started mopping the floor.

We straightened out a story on the way down, and I disappeared out of the car while my father went inside and got a couple of orderlies out with a stretcher.

Ambulances came and went, sirens blaring, lights flashing. A lot of uniforms about. By this time we were fighting the Brits as well as the Yanks. After a few minutes Malcolm returned, and I stepped out of the shadows and slid into the car.

"They bought it," he said. He lit a cigarette and coughed horribly. "Back to the house for a minute? Talk to your mother?"

"Dangerous for us all," I said. "If you could drop me off up at Barr's Cottage, I'd appreciate it. Otherwise, I'll hop out now."

"I'll take you."

Past the station again, at a more sedate pace.

"Thank you," I said, belatedly. "For everything."

He grinned, keeping his eye on the road. "'First, do no harm,'" he said. "Sort of thing."

He drove in silence for a minute, around the roundabout and out along Inverkip Road. The walls and high trees of the cemetery passed on the right. Gordon was probably picking his way through the middle of it by now.

"I'll give her your love," he said. "Yes?"

"Yes," I said.

"Won't be seeing you again for another couple of years?"

"If that," I answered, bleakly if honestly.

He turned off short of Barr's Cottage, into a council estate, and pulled in, under a broken streetlamp. The glow from another cigarette lit his face.

"All right," he said. "I have something to tell you."

Another sigh, another bout of coughing.

"You may not see me again. Your mother doesn't know this yet, but I've got six months. If that."

"Oh, God," I said.

"Cancer of the lung," he said. "Lot of it about. Filthy air around here." He crushed out the cigarette. "Stick to rural guerrilla warfare in future, old chap. It's healthier than the urban variety."

"I'll fight where I'm—"

His face blurred. I sobbed on his shoulder.

"Enough," he said. He held me away, gently.

"There's no pain," he assured me. "Whisky, tobacco, and heroin, three great blessings. And as the Greek said, nothing is terrible when you know that being nothing is not terrible. I'll know when to ease myself out."

"Oh, God," I said again, very inaptly.

His yellow teeth glinted. "I have no worries about meeting my maker. But, ah, I do have something on my conscience. A monkey on my back, which I want to offload on yours."

"All right," I said.

He leaned back and closed his eyes.

"Another time I treated a leg with a very similar injury . . ." he said. "You were there then, too. You were much smaller, and so was the patient. You do remember?"

"Of course," I said. My knees were shaking.

His eyes opened and he stared out through the windscreen.

"The last time we discussed this," he said, "I suggested that you look into the origin of the bomber. No doubt you have read some books, given the matter thought, and drawn your own conclusions."

"Yes," I said, "I certainly have, it's a—"

He held up one hand. "Keep it," he said. "I've had a lot longer to think about the origin of the pilot. My first thought was the same as yours, that it was a child. Then, when I got, ah, a closer look, I must confess that my second thought was that I was seeing the work of . . . another Mengele. The grey skin, the four digits on hands and feet, the huge eyes, the coppery colour of the blood . . . I thought for years that this was the result of some perverted Nazi science, you know. But, like you, I've read a great deal since. And as a medical man, I know what can and can't be done. No rare syndrome, no surgery, no mutation, no foul tinkering with the germ-plasm could have made that body. It was not a deformed human body. It was a perfectly healthy, normal body, but it was not human."

He turned to me, shaking his head. "The memory plays tricks, of course. But in retrospect, and even taking that into account, I believe that the pilot was not only not human, but not mammalian. I'm not even sure that he was a *vertebrate*. The bones in the leg were—"

His cheek twitched. "Like broken plastic, and hollow. Thin-walled, and filled with rigid tubes and struts rather than spongy bone and marrow."

I felt like giggling.

"You're saying the pilot was from *another planet*?"

"No," he said, sharply. "I'm not. I'm telling you what I *saw*." He waved a hand, his cigarette tip tracing a jiggly red line. "For all I know, the pilot may be a specimen of some race of intelligent beings that evolved on Earth and lurks unseen in the depths of the fucking Congo, or the Himalayas, like the Abominable Snowman!"

He laughed, setting off another wheezing cough.

"So there it is, John. A secret I won't be taking to the grave."

We talked a bit more, and then I got out of the car and watched the tail-lights disappear around a corner.

• • •

Scotland is not a good country for rural guerrilla warfare, having been long since stripped of trees and peasants. Without physical or social shelter, any guerrilla band in the hills and glens would be easily spotted and picked off, if they hadn't starved first. The great spaces of the Highlands were militarily irrelevant anyway.

So everybody believed, until the guerrilla war. Night, clouds and rain, gullies, boulders, bracken, isolated clumps of trees, the few real forests, burns and bridges and bothies all provided cover. The relatively sparse population could do little to betray us and—voluntarily or otherwise—much to help, and supplied few targets for enemy reprisals against civilians. Deer, sheep and rabbits abounded, edible wild plants and berries grew everywhere, and vegetables were easily enough bought or stolen. The strategic importance of the coastline and the offshore oilfields, and the vulnerability and propaganda value of the larger towns—Fort William, Inverness, Aberdeen, Thurso—compelled the state's armed forces to hold the entire enormous area: to move troops and armour along the long, narrow moorland roads, through glens ideal for ambush, and to fly low over often-clouded hills; to guard hydroelectric power stations, railways, microwave relay masts, the military's own installations and training-grounds; to patrol hundreds of miles of pipelines and cables.

That was just the Highlands: the area where I was, for obvious reasons, sent. Those who fought in the Borders, the Pentlands, the Southwest, and even the rich farmland of Perthshire all discovered other options, other opportunities. And that is to say nothing of what the English and Welsh comrades were doing. By 1981 the Front was making the country burn. The line had changed—Deng Hsiao-Ping was making cautious advances in the Versailles negotiations—but the fighting continued and we felt proud that we had fulfilled the late Chairman's directive. We had brought home the war.

●　●　●

The Bren was heavy and the pack was heavier. I was almost grateful that I had to move slowly. Moving under cloud cover was frustrating and dangerous. Visibility that October morning was a couple of metres; the clouds were down to about a hundred, and there was a storm on the way. Behind me nine men followed in line, down from the ridge. I found the bed of a burn, just a trickle at that moment, its boulders and pebbles slick and slippery from the rain of a week earlier. We made our way down this treacherous stairway from the invisible skyline we'd crossed. The first *glomach* I slipped into soaked me to the thighs.

I waded out and moved on. My ankle would have hurt if it hadn't been so cold. The light brightened and quite suddenly I was below the cloud layer, looking down at the road and the railway line at the bottom of the glen, and off to my right and to the west, a patch of meadow on the edge of a small loch with a crannog in the middle. Three houses, all widely separated, were visible up and down the glen. We knew who lived there, and they knew we knew. There would be no trouble from them. Just ahead of us was a ruined barn, a rectangle of collapsed drystone walling within which rowans grew and rusty sheets of fallen corrugated iron roofing sheltered nettles and brambles.

We'd come down at the right place. A couple of hundred metres to the left, a railway bridge crossed the road at an awkward zigzag bend. The bridge had been mined the previous night; the detonation cable should be snaking back to the ruined barn. A train was due in an hour and ten minutes. Our job was to bring down the bridge, giving the train just enough time to stop—civilian casualties weren't necessary for this operation. We intended to levy a revolutionary tax on the passengers and any valuable goods in transit before turning them out on the road and sending the empty train over where the bridge had been, thus blocking the road and railway and creating an ambush chokepoint for any soldiers or cops who sent to the scene. Booby-trapping the wreckage would be gravy, if we had the time.

I waved forward next man behind me, and he did likewise, and one by one we all emerged from the fog and hunkered down behind the lip of a shallow gully. Andy and Gordon were there, they'd been with me since the street-fighting days in Greenock. Of the others, three—Sandy and Mike and Neil—were also from Clydeside and four were local (from our point of view—in their own eyes Ian from Strome and Murdo from Torridon and Donald from Ullapool and Norman from Inverness were almost as distinct from each other in their backgrounds as they were from ours.)

"Tormod," I said to Norman, "you go and check out the bothy there, give us a wave if the electrician has done his job right. Two if he hasn't. Lie low and wait for the signal."

"There's no signal."

"The fucking whistle. My whistle."

"Oh, right you are."

Crouching, he ran to the ruin, and waved once after a minute. I sent Andy half a mile up the line to the nearest cutting, with a walkie-talkie, ready to confirm that the train had passed, and deployed the others on both sides of the bridge and both sides of the road. Apart from watching for any premature trouble, and being ready to raid the train when it had stopped, they were to stop any civilian vehicles that might chance to go under the bridge at the wrong moment. A light drizzle began to fall, and a front of heavier rain was marching up the glen from the west. Still about five miles distant, but with a good blow behind it, the opening breezes of which were already chilling my wet legs.

I had just settled myself and the Bren and the walkie-talkie behind a boulder on the hillside overlooking the bridge, with half an hour to spare before the train was due to pass at 12:11, when I heard the sound of a train far up the glen to the east. I couldn't see it, none of us could, except maybe Andy. I called him up.

"Passenger train," he said. "Wait a minute, it's got a couple of goods wagons at the back—shit, no! It's low-loaders! They've carrying two tanks!"

"Troop train," I guessed. "Maybe. Confirm when it passes."

"I can check it frae here wi the glasses."

He did, but still couldn't be certain.

Two minutes crawled by. The sound of the train filled the glen, or seemed to, until a sheep bleated nearby, startlingly loud. The radio crackled.

"Confirmed brown job," said Andy, just as the train emerged from the cutting and into view. It wasn't travelling very fast, maybe just over twenty miles per hour.

I had a choice. I could let this one pass, and continue with the operation, or I could seize this immensely dangerous chance to wreak far more havoc than we'd planned.

I watched the train pass below me, waited until the engine had crossed the bridge, and blew the whistle. Norman didn't hesitate. The blast came when the third carriage of the train was on the bridge. It utterly failed to bring the bridge down, but it threw that carriage upwards and sideways, off the rails. It ploughed through the bridge parapet and its front end crashed on to the road. The remaining four carriages concertina'd into its rear end. One of them rolled on to the embankment, the one behind that was derailed, and the two tank-transporting flatbeds remained on the track.

The engine, and the two front carriages, had by this time travelled a quarter of a mile further down the track, and were accelerating rapidly away. There was nothing that could be done about that. I opened fire at once on the wreck, raking the bursts along the carriage windows. The rest of the squad followed up, then, like myself, they must have ducked down to await return fire.

In the silence that followed the crash and the firing, other noises gradually became audible. Among the screams and yells from the wreckage were the shouts of command. Within seconds a spatter of rifle and pistol fire started up. I raised my head cautiously, watched for the flashes, and directed single shots from the Bren in their direction.

Silence again. Neil and Murdo reported in on the walkie-talkie from the other side of the track, and up ahead a bit. They'd each hit one or two attempts at rescue work or flight. We seemed to have the soldiers on the train pinned down. At the same time it was difficult for us to break cover ourselves. In any sustained exchange of fire we were likely to be the first to run out of ammunition, and then to be picked off as we ran.

This impasse was brought to an end after half an hour by a torrential downpour and a further descent of the clouds. The scheduled train, either cancelled or forewarned, hadn't arrived. Any cars arriving at the scene had backed off and turned away, unmolested by us. We regrouped by the roadside, west of the bridge, well within earshot of the carriage that had crashed on the road.

"This is murder," said Norman.

I was well aware of the many lives my decision had just ended or wrecked. I had no compunction about that, being even more aware of how many lives we had saved at the troops' destination.

"Seen any white flags, have you?" I snarled. "Until you do, we're still fighting."

"Only question is," said Andy, "do we pull back now while we're ahead?"

"There'll be rescue and reinforcement coming for sure," said Murdo. "The engine could come steaming back any minute, for one thing."

"They're probably overestimating us," I said, thinking aloud in the approved democratic manner. "I mean, who'd be mad enough to attack a troop train with ten men?"

We laughed, huddled in the pouring rain. The windspeed was increasing by the minute.

"There'll be no air support in this muck," said Sandy.

"All the same," I said, "our best bet is to pull out now, we have the chance and there's nothing more to—wait a minute. What about the tanks?"

"Can't do much damage to them," said Mike.

"Aye," I said, "but think of the damage we can do *with* them."

• • •

It was easy. It was ridiculously, pathetically, trivially easy. Four of us had National Service experience with tanks, so we split into two groups and after firing a few shots to keep the enemy's heads down we knocked the shackles off the chains and commandeered both tanks. They were fuelled and armed, ready for action. We crashed them off the sides of the flatbeds and drove them perilously down the steep slope to the road, shelled the train, drove under the bridge, shelled the train again, then shelled the bridge. Then we drove over the tracks and around the back of the now-collapsed bridge and a couple of miles up the road, and off to one side, and when the relief column arrived—a dozen troop trucks and four armoured cars—we started shelling that.

By midafternoon we'd inflicted hundreds of casualties and had the remaining troops and vehicles completely pinned down. Reinforcements from our side began to arrive, pouring fire from the ridges into the glen, raiding more weapons and ammunition from the train and the relief column; and then attacking *its* relief column. The battle of Glen Carron was turning into the biggest engagement of the war in the British Isles. The increasingly appalling weather was entirely to our advantage, although my squad, at least, were on the point of pneumonia from the soaking we'd got earlier.

The first we knew of the bomber's arrival was when we lost contact with the men on the ridge. A minute later, I saw through the periscope the other tank—a few hundred metres away at the time—take a direct hit. That erupting flash of earth and metal told me without a doubt that Gordon was dead, along with Ian, Mike, Sandy and Norman.

"Reverse reverse reverse!" I shouted.

Murdo slammed us into reverse gear and hit the accelerator, throwing me painfully forward as we shot up a slope and into a birch-screened gully. The tank lurched upward as the bomb missed us by about twenty metres, then crashed back down on its tracks.

Blood poured from my brow and lip.

"Everybody all right?" I yelled.

No reply. Silence. I looked down and saw Andy tugging my leg, mouthing and nodding. He pointed to his ears. I grimaced acknowledgement and looked again through the periscope and saw the bomber descend towards the road just across the glen from us, by one of the trapped columns. Five hundred metres away, and exactly level with us.

There was a shell in the chamber. I swivelled the turret and racked the gun as hearing returned through a raging ringing in my ears, just in time to be deafened again as I fired. My aim was by intuition, with no use of the sights, pure Zen like a perfect throw of a stone. I knew it was going to hit, and it did.

The bomber shot upwards, skimmed towards us, then fluttered down to settle athwart the river at the bottom of the glen, just fifty metres away and ten metres below us, lying there like a fucking enormous landmine in our path.

I poked Murdo's shoulder with my foot and he engaged the forward gear. Andy set up a bit of suppressing fire with the machine-gun. We slewed to a halt beside the bomber. I grabbed a Bren, threw open the hatch and clambered through and jumped down. My ears were still ringing. The wind was fierce, the rain an instant skin-soaking, the wind-chill terrible. Water poured off the bomber like sea off a surfacing submarine. There was a smell of peatbog and metal and crushed myrtle. Smoke drifted from a ragged notch in its edge, similar to the one on the crippled bomber I'd seen all those years ago.

I walked around the bomber, warily leaping past the snouts of machine-guns in its rim. With the Bren's butt I banged the hatch. The thing rang like a bell, even louder than my tinnitus.

The hatch opened. I stood back and levelled the Bren. A big visored helmet emerged, then long arms levered up a torso, and then the hips and legs swung up and out. The pilot slid down the side of the bomber and stood in front of me, arms raised high. Very slowly, the hands went to the helmet and lifted it off.

A cascade of blonde hair shook loose. The pilot was incredibly beautiful and she was about seven feet tall.

•••

We left the tank sabotaged and blocking the road about five miles to the west, and took off into the hills. Through the storm and the gathering dusk we struggled to a lonely safe-house, miles from anywhere. Our prisoner was tireless and silent. Her flying-suit was dark green and black, to all appearances standard for an American pilot, right down to the badges. She carried her helmet and knotted her hair deftly at her nape. Her Colt .45 and Bowie knife she surrendered without protest.

The safe house was a gamekeeper's lodge, with a kitchen and a couple of rooms, the larger of which had a fireplace. Dry wood was stacked on the hearth. We started the fire and stripped off our wet clothes—all of our clothes—and hung them about the place, then one by one we retrieved dry clothes from the stash in the back room. The prisoner observed us without a blink, and removed her own flying-suit. Under it she was wearing a closer-fitting garment of what looked like woven aluminium, with tubes running under its surface. It covered a well-proportioned female body. Too well-proportioned, indeed, for the giant she was. She sprawled on the worn armchair by the fire and looked at us, still silent, and carefully untied her wet hair and let it fall down her back.

Murdo, Andy, Neil and Donald huddled in front of the fire. I stood behind them, holding the prisoner's pistol.

"Donald," I said, "you take the first look-out. You'll find oilskins in the back. Neil, make some tea, and give it to Donald first."

"Three sugars, if we have it," said Donald, getting up and padding through to the other room. Neil disappeared into the kitchen. Sounds of him fiddling with and cursing the little gas stove followed. The prisoner smiled, for the first time. Her pale features were indeed beautiful, but somewhat angular, almost masculine; her eyes were a distinct violet, and very large.

"Talk," I told her.

"Jodelle Smith," she said. "Flight-Lieutenant. Serial number . . ." She rattled it off.

The voice was deep, for a woman, but soft, the American accent perfect. Donald gave her a baleful glare as he headed for the door and the storm outside it.

"All right," I said. "We are not signatories to the Geneva Convention. We do not regard you as a prisoner of war, but as a war criminal, an air pirate. You have one chance of being treated as a prisoner of war, with all the rights that go with that, and that is to answer all our questions. Otherwise, we will turn you over to the nearest revolutionary court. They're pretty biblical around here. They'll probably stone you to death."

I don't know how the lads kept a straight face through all that. Perhaps it was the anger and grief over the loss of our friends and comrades, the same feeling that came out in my own voice. I could indeed have wished her dead, but otherwise I was bluffing—there were no revolutionary courts in the region, and anyway our policy with prisoners was to disarm them, attempt to interrogate them, and turn them loose as soon as it was safe to do so.

The pilot sat silent for a moment, head cocked slightly to one side, then shrugged and smiled.

"Other bomber pilots have been captured," she said. "They've all been recovered unharmed." She straightened up in the chair, and leaned forward. "If you're not satisfied with the standard name, rank, and serial number, I'm happy to talk to you about anything other than military secrets. What would you like to know?"

I glanced at the others. I had never shared my father's story, or my own, with any of them, and I was glad of that now because the appearance of this pilot would have discredited it. Compared with what my father had described, she looked human. Compared with most people, she looked very strange.

"Where do you really come from?" I asked.

"Venus," she said.

The others all laughed. I didn't.

"What happened to the other kind of pilots?" I asked. I held out one hand about a metre above the ground, as though patting a child's head.

"Oh, we took over from the Martians a long time ago," she told us earnestly. "They're still involved in the war, of course, but they're not on the front line anymore. The Americans found their appearance disconcerting, and concealing them became too much of a hassle."

I glared down the imminent interruptions from my men.

"You're saying there are two alien species fighting on the American side?"

"Yes," she said. She laughed suddenly. "Greys are from Mars, blondes are from Venus."

"Total fucking *cac*," said Neil. "She's a Yank. They're always tall. Better food."

"Maybe she is," I said, "but she is not the kind of pilot I was expecting. And I've seen one of the other kind. My father saw it up close."

The woman's eyebrows went up.

"The Aird incident? 1964?"

I nodded.

"Ah," she said. "Your father must be . . . Dr. Malcolm Donald Matheson, and you are his son, John."

"How the hell do you know that?"

"I've read the reports."

"This is insane," said Andy. "It's some kind of trick, it's a trap. We shouldnae say another word, or listen tae any."

"There's eggs and bacon and tatties in the kitchen," I said. "See if you can make yourself useful."

He glowered at me and stalked out.

"But he's right, you know," I said, loud enough for Andy to overhear. "We are going to have to send you up a level or two, for interrogation, as soon as the storm passes. Will you still talk then?"

She spread her hands. "On the same basis as I've spoken to you, yes. No military secrets."

"Aye, just disinformation," said Murdo. "You're not telling us that it wouldn't be a military secret if the Yanks really were getting help from *outer space*? But making people believe it, now, that would be worth something. Christ, it's enough of a job fighting the Americans. Who would fight the fucking Martians?"

He leaned back and laughed harshly.

The woman who called herself Jodelle gazed at him with narrowed, thoughtful eyes.

"There is that argument," she said. "There is the other argument, that if the Communists could claim the real enemy was not human they would unite even more people against the Allied side, and that the same knowledge would create all kinds of problems—political, religious, philosophical—for Allied morale. So far, the latter argument has prevailed."

My grip tightened on the pistol.

"You are talking about psychological warfare," I said. "And you are doing it, right here, now. Shut the fuck up."

She gave us a pert smile and shrug.

"No more talking to her," I said.

My own curiosity was burning me inside, but I knew that to pursue the conversation—with the mood here as it was—really would be demoralising and confusing. I got everybody busy guarding the prisoner, cleaning weapons, laying the table. Andy brought through plate laden with steaming, fragrant thick bacon and fried eggs and boiled potatoes. I relieved Donald on the outside watch before taking a bite myself, and prowled around in the howling wet dark with my M-16 under the oilskin cape and my belly grumbling. The window blinds were keeping the light in all right, and only the wind-whipped smoke from the chimney could betray our presence. I kept my closest attention to downwind, where someone might smell it. There was no chance of anyone seeing it.

I was looking that way, peering and listening intently through the dark to the east, when I felt a prickle in the back of my neck and smelled something electric.

I turned with a sort of reluctance, as though expecting to see a ghost. What I saw was a bomber, haloed in blue, descending between me and the house. There might have been a fizzing sound, or that may be just a memory of the hissing rain. For a moment I stood as still as the bomber, which floated preternaturally above the ground. Then I raised the rifle. Something flashed out from the bomber, and I was knocked backwards, and senseless.

● ● ●

I woke to voices, and pain. My skin smarted all over; my eyelids hurt to open. I was lying on my side on a slightly yielding smooth grey floor. The light was pearly and sourceless. Moving slightly, I found I had some bruises and what felt like scrapes on my back, but apart from that and the burning feeling everything seemed to be fine. My oilskins were gone, as were my weapons and, curiously enough, my watch. I raised my head, propped myself on one elbow and looked around. The room I lay in was circular, about fifteen metres across. My comrades were lying beside me, unconscious, looking sunburned, but breathing normally and apparently uninjured. There was a sort of bench or shelf around the room, which in one section looped away from the wall to form a seat, at which a tall person with long fair hair sat with their back to me, hands on a pair of knobbed levers. Other parts of the shelf were not padded seating but tables and odd panels. Above the bench was a black screen or window which likewise encircled the room.

Sitting on the bench, on either side of the person I guessed was the pilot, were three similar people—one of them, just then noticing that I was stirring, being the woman we'd captured—and a small creature with a large head, slit mouth, tiny nostrils and enormous black eyes. Its skin was grey, but somehow not an unhealthy grey—it had a glow to it, a visible warmth underneath; though hairless it reminded me of the skin of a seal. Its legs were short, its arms long, and its hands—I recalled my father's words, and felt a slight thrill at their confirmation—bore four long digits.

It too noticed me, and it looked directly at me and—it didn't blink, something flicked sideways across its eyes, like an eagle's. The woman stood up and stepped over and stood looking down at me.

"There's no need to be afraid of the Martian," she said.

"I'm not afraid," I said, then caught myself. "John Matheson, unit commander, MB 246."

She reached down, took my hand and hauled me to my feet, without effort. There was something wrong about my weight. I felt curiously light.

"Your friends will wake up shortly," she said. "OK, consider yourself a prisoner of war if you like, but there's no need to not be civil. We have nothing to hide from you anymore, and we really don't have anything we want to find out from you."

I said nothing. She pointed to the bench.

"Relax," she said, "sit down, have a coffee." Then she giggled, in a very disarming way. "'For you, Johnny, the vor iss over.'"

Her fake, Ealing-studio German accent was as perfect as her genuine-sounding American one. I couldn't forbear to smile back, and walked over to the seat. On the way I stumbled a little. It was like the top step that isn't there.

"Martian gravity," Jodelle said, steadying me. The Martian bowed his big head slightly, as though in apology. I sat down beside one of the other people, the "Venusians" as I perforce mentally labelled them. All except Jodelle were evidently male, though their hair was as long and fair as hers. One of them passed me a mug of coffee; out of the corner of my eye, I noticed a coffee pot and electric kettle on one of the table sections, and some mugs and, banally enough, a kilogramme packet of Tate & Lyle sugar.

"My name is Soren," the man said. He waved towards the others. "The pilot is Olaf, and the man next to him is Harold."

"And my name is Chuck," said the Martian. His small shoulders shrugged. "That's what I'm called around here, anyway." His voice was like that of a tough wee boy, his accent American, but he sounded like he was speaking a learned second language.

I nodded at them all and said nothing, gratefully sipping the coffee. Outside, the view was completely black, though the movements of the pilot's eyes, head, and hands appeared to be responding to some visible exterior environment.

One by one, Neil, Donald, Murdo and Andy came round, and went through the same process of disorientation, astonishment, reassurance and suspicion as I had. We ended up sitting together, not speaking to each other or to our captors, perhaps silently mourning the loss of our comrades and friends in the other tank. The bomber's crew talked among themselves in a language I did not recognise, and attended to instruments. None of us was in anything but a hostile mood, and if the aliens had been less unknown in their intentions and capabilities we might have regarded their evident unconcern as an opportunity to try to overwhelm them, rather than—as we tacitly acknowledged—evidence that they had no reason to fear us.

After about half an hour, they relaxed, and all sat down on the long seat.

"Almost there," Jodelle Smith said.

Before any of us could respond, one side of the encircling window filled with the glare of the sun, instantly dimmed by some property of the display; the other with the light of that same sun reflected on white clouds, of which I glimpsed a dazzling, visibly curved expanse a second before we plunged into them. Moments later we were underneath them, and a green surface spread below us. Looking up, I could see the silvery underside of the clouds. Our rapid descent soon brought the green surface into focus as an apparently endless forest, broken by lakes and rivers, and by plateaus or gentler rises covered with grass. After a few seconds we were low enough for the shadow of the bomber to be visible, skimming across the treetops. The circle of shade enlarged, and then disappeared. I blinked, and saw that we were now stationary above a broad valley bounded by high sandstone cliffs and divided by a wide, meandering river.

Then, with a yawing motion which we could see but not feel—so it seemed that the landscape swayed, and not the ship—we descended, and settled on a grassy plain. Around us, in the middle distance, were rows of Nissen huts; in the farther distance, watchtowers and barbed wire.

"Welcome to Venus," said the pilot.

• • •

The camp held about a thousand people, from all over the world. Most of them were Front soldiers or cadre. There were as many women as there were men, and there were some children. The Front basically ran the camp, through committees of the various national sections, and an international committee for which the main qualification seemed to be fluency in Russian. The only rule that the Venusians enforced was a curfew and blackout between sunset and sunrise. They didn't bother about which hut you spent the night in, so long as you were in a hut.

They gave us no work to do, and watched unconcerned as we practised drill and unarmed combat, sweltering in the heat and humidity. Food and drink were adequate, and in fact more varied and nutritious than the fare to which most of the inmates, including myself, had become accustomed. This is not to say that our confinement was pleasant. The continuous cloud cover felt like a great shining lid pressing down on us, day after day. Every day it seemed to, or perhaps actually did, descend a little lower. The nightly lock-downs were hellish, even though the huts did in fact cool down somewhat. The wire around the camp was almost equally suffocating, one we'd realised that it wasn't so much there to keep us in as to keep the dinosaurs out. The same was true of the guards' strange weapons, which could—if turned to a much higher setting than was ever used against prisoners—fire bolts of electricity or plasma sufficient to turn back even the biggest of the great blundering beasts which flocked to the river every couple of days, their feet making the plain shake. We called them dinosaurs, because they resembled the reconstructions of dinosaurs which most of us had seen in books, but I knew from my scientific education that they could not be dinosaurs—they were too vigorous, too obviously hot-blooded, to be the sluggish reptilian giants of the Triassic and Jurassic eras. Whatever they may have been, their presence certainly discouraged attempts to escape.

The British contingent was in two Nissen huts: twenty men in one, twenty women in the other. They had a committee of three men, three women, and a chairman, and they spent a lot of time trying to regulate sexual relations. It was all very British and messy, uncomfortably between the strict puritanism of the Chinese comrades and the easygoing, if occasionally violent, mores of the Latin Americans and Africans. My unit decided to ignore all that and do what we considered the proper British thing.

We set up an escape committee.

● ● ●

"What the hell are you doing, Matheson?"

I waved my free hand. "Just a minute—"

It didn't interrupt my counting. When I'd finished, I put the one-metre line and the 250-gramme tin of peas on the table and glanced over my calculations before looking up at Purdie. The young Englishman was on our hut committee and the camp committee, but not the escape committee, which he regarded as a diversion in both senses of the word.

"We're not on Venus," I said.

He glanced over his shoulder, as if to confirm that we were still alone in the hut, then sat on a corner of the table.

"How d'you figure that out?"

"Pendulum swing," I said. "Galileo's experiment. The gravity here is exactly the same as on Earth. Venus has about eighty percent of the mass of Earth."

"Hmm," he said. "Well done. Most people begin by wondering why nothing feels lighter, and then put it down to our muscles adapting to the supposed lower gravity. Still, can't say it's a surprise, old chap. Some of us reckon they keep us in at night because if we went outside we could see the moon through the cloud cover, and even the least educated of us is aware that Venus doesn't *have* a bloody moon."

"So where are we?" I waved a hand. "It seems a wee bit out of the way, if this is Earth."

He crooked one leg over the other and lit a cigarette.

"Well, the camp committee has considered that. The usual explanation is that we're in some unexplored region of a South American jungle, something like what's-his-name's *The Lost World*."

"Conan Doyle," I said automatically. I screwed up my eyes against the smoke and the glaring light from the open door of the hut. "Doesn't seem likely to me."

"Me neither," said Purdie cheerfully. "For one thing, the midday sun isn't high enough in the sky for this to be a tropical latitude, but it's *bloody* hot. Any other ideas?"

"What if instead we're in somewhere out of *The Time Machine*? Well, you know . . . *dinosaurs*?"

Purdie frowned and probed in his ear with a finger.

"That has come up. Our Russian comrades shot it down in flames. Time travel is ruled out by dialectical materialism, I gather. But I must say, this place does strike me as frightfully Cretaceous, the anomaly of hot-blooded dinosaurs aside. My personal theory is that we're on a planet around another star, which resembles Earth in the Cretaceous period."

He cracked a smile. "That, however, implies a vastly more advanced civilization which either isn't communist or *is* communist and fights on the side of the imperialists. Neither of which are acceptable speculations to the, ah, leading comrades here, who thus stick with the line that the self-styled Venusians and Martians are the spawn of Nazi medical experiments, or some such."

"Bollocks," I said.

Purdie shrugged. "You may well say that, but I wouldn't. I myself am troubled by the thought that my own theory at least strongly suggests—even if it doesn't, strictly speaking, require—faster-than-light travel, which is ruled out by Einstein—an authority who to me carries more weight on matters of physics than Engels or Lenin, I'm afraid."

"Relativity doesn't rule out time travel," I said. "Even if dialectical materialism does."

"And no science whatever rules out lost-world relict dinosaur populations," said Purdie. He shrugged. "Occam's razor and all that, keeps up morale, so lost-world is the official line."

"First I've heard of it," I said. "Nobody's even suggested we're not on Venus in the two weeks I've been here."

"Bit of a test, comrade," he said dryly. He stubbed out his cigarette, hopped off the table and stuck out his right hand for me to shake. "Congratulations on passing it. Now, how would you like to join the *real* escape committee?"

• • •

The official escape committee had long since worked through and discarded the laughable expedients—tunnels, gliders and so on—which I and my mates, perhaps overinfluenced by such tales of derring-do as *The Colditz Story* and *The Wooden Horse*, had earnestly evaluated. The only possibility was for a mass break-out, exploiting the only factor of vulnerability we could see in the camp's defences, and one which itself was implicitly part of them: the dinosaur herds. It would also exploit the fact that, as far as we knew, the guards were reluctant to use lethal force on prisoners. So far, at least, they'd only ever turned on us the kind of electrical shock which had knocked out me and my team, and indeed most people here at the time of their capture or subsequent resistance.

The tedious details of how a prison-camp escape attempt is prepared have been often enough recounted in the genre of POW memoirs referred to above, and need not be repeated here. Suffice it to say that about fifty days after my arrival, the preparations were complete. From then on, all those involved in the scheme waited hourly for the approach of a suitably large herd, and on the second day of our readiness, conveniently soon after breakfast, one arrived.

About a score of the great beasts: bulls, cows, and calves, their tree-trunk-thick legs striding across the plain, their tree-top-high heads swaying to sniff and stooping to browse, were marching straight towards the eastern fence of the camp, which lay athwart their route to the river. The guards were just bestirring themselves to rack up the setting on their plasma rifles when the riot started.

At the western end of the camp a couple of Chinese women started screaming, and on this cue scores of other prisoners rushed to surround them and pile in to a highly realistic and noisy fight. Guards from the perimeter patrol raced towards them, and were immediately turned on and overwhelmed by a further crowd that just kept on coming, leaping or stepping over those who'd fallen to the low-level electric blasts. At that the guards from the watchtowers on that side began to descend, some of them firing.

My team was set for the actual escape, not the diversion. I was crouched behind the door of our hut with Murdo, Andy, Neil, Donald and a dozen others, including Purdie. We'd grabbed our stashed supplies and our improvised tools, and now awaited our chance. Another human wave assault, this time a crowd of Russians heading for the fence where the guards were belatedly turning to face the oncoming dinosaurs, thundered past. We dashed out behind them and ran for an empty food-delivery truck, temporarily unguarded. It even had a plasma-rifle, which I instantly commandeered, racked inside.

The Russians swarmed up the wire, standing on each others shoulders like acrobats. The guards, trying to deal with them and the dinosaurs, failed to cope with both. A bull dinosaur brought down the fence and two watchtowers, and by the time he'd been himself laid low with concerted plasma fire, we'd driven over the remains of the fence and hordes of prisoners were fleeing in every direction.

Within minutes the first bombers arrived, skimming low, rounding up the escapees. They missed us, perhaps because they'd mistaken the truck—a very standard U.S. Army Dodge—for one of their own. We abandoned it at the foot of the cliffs, scaled them in half an hour of frantic scrambling up corries and chimneys, and by the time the bombers came looking for us we'd disappeared into the trees.

• • •

Heat, damp, thorns, and very large dragonflies. Apart from that last and the small dinosaur-like animals—some, to our astonishment, with feathers—scuttling through the undergrowth, the place didn't look like another planet, or even the remote past. Since my knowledge of what the remote past was supposed to look like was derived entirely from dim memories of *Look and Learn* and slightly fresher memories of a stroll through the geological wing of the Hunterian Museum, Glasgow, this wasn't saying much. I vaguely expected giant ferns and cycads and so forth, and found perfectly recognisable conifers, oaks and maples. The flowers were less instantly recognisable, but didn't look particularly primitive, or exotic.

I shared these thoughts with Purdie, who laughed.

"You're thinking of the Carboniferous, old chap," he said. "This is all solidly Cretaceous, so far."

"Could be modern," I said.

"Apart from the animals," he pointed out, as though this wasn't obvious. "And as I said, it's not tropical, but it's too bloody hot to be a temperate latitude."

I glanced back. Our little column was plodding along behind us. We were heading in an approximately upward direction, on a reasonably gentle slope.

"I've thought about this," I said. "What if this whole area is some kind of artificial reserve in *North* America? If it's possible to genetically . . . engineer, I suppose would be the word . . . different kinds of humans, why shouldn't it be possible to do the same with birds and lizards and so on, and make a sort of botched copy of dinosaurs?"

"And keep it all under some vast artificial cloud canopy?" He snorted. "You overestimate the imperialists, let alone the Nazi scientists, comrade."

"Maybe we're under a huge dome," I said, not entirely seriously. I looked up at the low sky, which seemed barely higher than the tree-tops. It really had become lower since we'd arrived. "Buckminster Fuller had plans that were less ambitious than that."

Purdie wiped sweat from his forehead with the back of his hand. "Now that," he said, "is quite a plausible suggestion. It sure *feels* like we're in a bloody greenhouse. Mind you, none of us saw anything like that, from the bomber."

"That was a screen, not a window."

"Hmm. A remarkably realistic screen, in that case. Back to implausibly advanced technology."

We wouldn't have to speculate for long, because our course was taking us directly up to the cloud level, which we reached within an hour or so. I assigned my lads the task of guiding the others, who were quite unfamiliar with the techniques of low-visibility walking, and we all headed on up. First wisps, then dense damp billows, of fog surrounded us. I led the way and moved forward cautiously, whistling signals back and forth. Behind me I could just see Purdie and two of the English women comrades. Underfoot the ground became grassier, and around us the trees became shorter and the bushes more sparse. The only way to follow a particular direction was to go upslope, and that—with a few inevitable wrong turnings that led us into declivities— we did.

The fog thinned. Clutching the plasma rifle, hoping I had correctly figured out how to use it, I walked forward and up and into clear air. A breeze blew refreshingly into my face, and as I glanced back I saw that it had pushed back the fog and revealed all of our straggling party. We were on one of the wide, rounded hilltops I'd seen from the bomber. In the far distance I could see other green islands above the clouds. The sky was blue, the sun was bright.

All around us, people rose out of the long grass, aiming plasma rifles. I dropped mine and raised my hands.

About a hundred metres in front of us was the wire fence of another camp.

• • •

We went into the camp without resistance, but without being searched or, in my case, disarmed: I was told to pick up my rifle and sling it over my shoulder. The people were human beings like us, but they were weird. They spoke English, in strange accents and with a lot of unfamiliar words. Several of them were coloured or half-caste, but their accents were as English as those of the rest. I found myself walking beside a young woman with part of her hair dyed violet. I knew it was a dye because it was growing out: the roots were black. She had several rings and studs in her ear, and not just in the earlobe. She was wearing baggy grey trousers with pockets at the thighs, and a silky scarlet sleeveless top with a silver patch shaped like a rabbit. Around her bicep was a tattoo of thorns. Under her tarty make-up her face was quite attractive. Her teeth looked amazingly white and even, like an American's.

"My name's Tracy," she said. She had some kind of Northern English accent; I couldn't place it more than that. "You?"

Name, rank, serial number . . .

"Where you from?"

Name, rank, serial number . . .

"Forget that," she said. "You're not a prisoner."

A massive gate made from logs and barbed wire was being pushed shut behind us. Nissen huts inside a big square of fence, a bomber parked just outside it.

"Oh no?" I said.

"Keeps the fucking dinosaurs out, dunnit?"

Somebody handed me a tin mug of tea, black with a lot of sugar. I sipped it and looked around. If this was a camp it was one where the prisoners had guns.

Or one run by trusties . . . I was still suspicious.

"Where are the aliens?" I asked.

"The what?"

"The Venusians, the Martians . . ." I held my free hand above my head, then at chest height.

Tracy laughed. "Is that what they told you?"

I nodded. "Not sure if I believe them, though."

She was still chuckling. "You lot must be from Commie World. Never built the rockets, right?"

"The Russians have rockets," I said, with some indignation. "The biggest in the world—they have a range of hundreds of kilometres!"

"Exactly. No ICBMs." She smiled at my frown. "Inter-Continental Ballistic Missiles. None of them, and no space-probes. Jeez. You could still half believe this might be Venus, with jungles and tall Aryans. And that the Greys are Martians."

"Well, what are they?" I asked, becoming irritated by her smug teasing.

"Time-travellers," she said. "From the future." She shivered slightly. "From *another* world's future. The ones you call the Venusians are from about half a million years up ahead of the twentieth century, the Greys're from maybe five million. In your world's twentieth century they fly bombers and fight commies. In mine they're just responsible for flying saucers, alien abductions, cattle mutilations and odd sock phenomena."

I let this incomprehensibility pass.

"So where are we now?"

I meant the camp. I knew where we were in general, but that was what she answered.

"This, Johnny-boy, is the past. They can never go back to the same future, but they can go back to the same place in the past, where they can make no difference. The common past, the past of us all—the Cretaceous."

She looked at me with a bit more sympathy. My companions were finishing off their tea and gazing around, looking as baffled and edgy as I felt. The other prisoners, if that was what they were, gathered around us seemed more alien than the bomber pilots.

"Come on," Tracy said, gesturing towards some rows of seats in front of which a table had been dragged. "Debriefing time. You have a lot to learn."

• • •

I have learned a lot.

I tug the reins and the big Clydesdale turns, and as I follow the plough around I see a porpoise leap in the choppy water of the Moray Firth. My hands and back are sore but I'm getting used to it, and the black soil here is rich, and arable after the trees have been cut down and their stumps dynamited. The erratic boulders have been cleared away long ago, by the long-dead first farmers of this land, and no glaciers have revisited it since its last farmers passed away. The rougher ground is pasture, grazed by half-wild long-horns, a rugged synthetic species. The village is stockaded on a hilltop nearby. We have no human enemies, but wolves, bears and lions prowl the forests and moors. We are not barbarians—the plough that turns the furrow I walk has an iron blade, and the revolver on my hip was made in Hartford, Connecticut, millennia ago and worlds away. The posthumans settled us—and other colonies—on this empty Earth with machinery and medicines, weapons and tools and libraries, and enough partly used ball-point pens to keep us all scribbling until our descendants can make their own.

On countless other empty Earths they have done the same. Somewhere unreachable, but close to hand, another man, perhaps another John Matheson, may be tramping a slightly different furrow. I wish him well.

There are many possible worlds, and in almost all of them humanity didn't survive the time from which most of us have been taken. Either the United States and the Soviet Union destroyed each other and the rest of civilization in an atomic war in the fifties or sixties, or they didn't, and the collapse of the socialist states in the late twentieth century so discredited socialism and international cooperation that humanity failed utterly to unite in time to forestall the environmental disasters of the twenty-first.

In a few, a very few possible worlds, enough scattered remnants of humanity survived as savages to eventually—hundreds of thousands of years later—become the ancestors of the posthuman species we called the Venusians. Who in turn—millions of years later—themselves gave rise to the posthuman clade we called the Martians. It was the latter who discovered time travel, and with it some deep knowledge about the future and past of the universe.

I don't pretend to understand it. As Feynman said—in a world where he didn't die in jail—it all goes back to the experiment with the light and the two slits, and Feynman himself didn't pretend to understand *that*. What we have been told is simply this—that the past of the universe, its very habitability for human beings, depends on its future being one—or rather, many—which contain as many human beings and their successors as possible, until the end of time.

It is not enough for the time-travellers to intervene in histories such as the one from which I come, and by defeating Communism while avoiding atomic war, save a swathe of futures for cooperation and survival. They also have to repopulate the time-lines in which humanity destroyed itself, and detonate new shock-waves of possibility that will spread humanity across time and forward through it, on an ever-expanding, widening front.

The big mare stops and looks at me, and whinnies. The sun is low above the hills to the west, the hills where I once—or many times—fought. Its light is red in the sky. The dust from the last atomic war is no longer dangerous, but it will linger in the high atmosphere for thousands of years to come.

I unharness the horse, heave the plough to the shed at the end of the field, and lead the beast up the hill towards the village. The atomic generator is humming, the lights are coming on, and dinner in the communal kitchen will soon be ready. Tracy will be putting away the day's books in the library, and yawning and stretching herself. Maybe this evening, after we've all eaten, she can be persuaded to tell us some stories. For me she has many fascinations—she's quite unlike any woman I've ever met—and the only one I'm happy for her to share with everybody else is her stories from the world where, I still feel, history turned out almost as it would have done without any meddling at all by the time-travellers: her world, the world where the prototype bomber didn't work; the world where, as she puts it, the Roswell saucer crashed.

OTHER DEVIATIONS: THE HUMAN FRONT EXPOSED

EVERY ALTERNATE HISTORY HAS implications, explicit or otherwise, for how we think (or how the author would have us think) about the course history actually took. Ward Moore's *Bring the Jubilee*, set in the 1960s of a history in which the South won the Civil War, shows us an America much less attractive and advanced than the one we know. Few stories in the apparently endless "Hitler Wins!" subgenre show us a better world than ours.

The Human Front is set in a world where the Soviet Union ceased to exist in 1949 or thereabouts, roughly forty years earlier than it actually did. The (literal) mechanism by which this happens is improbable, and I hope amusing, but irrelevant to the question of whether the resulting world is an improvement on the one we live in, and of whether it's a logical result of the change. In this case the moment of change—the Jonbar point, to use the skiffy jargon—is a frivolity, but the history that diverges from it isn't.

The reasoning behind Matheson's world goes like this: The Soviet Union is defeated and occupied in the late

1940s. Stalin survives as a figurehead of continuing resistance, and the Chinese Revolution takes place much as in our world, but this isn't enough to stop the old colonial powers hanging on to their possessions. Without a Soviet or Chinese nuclear deterrent, the West has a free hand to use nuclear weapons against the independence movements—as indeed was seriously contemplated in our own history. Without African and Asian independence, and the general inspiration of the colonial revolution, the Black movement in the U.S. arrives later and less powerfully. Jim Crow in the U.S., and the "colour bar" in the British Empire, remain. Other movements that in our world were influenced by the Black struggle, such as the uprising of the Catholics of Northern Ireland, never take off. The Communist movement, with no uncontested sovereign territory but China left to lose, and no divisions arising from the Sino-Soviet split and de-Stalinisation, retains its post–World War II militancy, and its global leadership passes to the most leftist wing of Chinese Communism, identified with Lin Piao. There's no Vietnam War in this world—instead, the world becomes Vietnam.

What this implies about how I see the world we actually live in is left as an exercise for the reader.

An alternate history usually begins with the question: what if some real historical event had happened differently? This story seeded itself from a different question: what if something that *didn't* happen had happened differently? I had in mind a particular event in 1947 that never happened, and that has become the foundation of a genuine modern myth. (You know what it was.) And that raised another question.

The other question, of course, was why on Earth should a flying saucer crash at all, let alone close to an Air Force base? One possible answer to that was obvious: the saucer was on a test flight, or—aha!—a demonstration flight, for the Air Force. If the well-known saucer crash (which didn't happen) *hadn't happened*—why then, the Pentagon would have gone ahead and ordered more of them! And used them to win the Cold War before it had got properly started!

But then—a whole different 1950s would have unfolded, and 1960s, and . . .

And there I left it, for several years. The weight of research needed to build such an elaborate alternate history struck me as too heavy for such a slender reed of a premise. It was only when Peter Crowther proposed that I write one of a projected series of novellas that I took the idea down and dusted it off. It still seemed that a lot of research would be required, even for a novella. As I pondered that, I had what I still think were my two best ideas about this story.

The first was that I didn't need to research the late 1950s and the 1960s, because I *remembered* them. The second was to write the story in the first person, as alternate autobiography. By following the track of my own life—born on the Isle of Lewis, moving to Greenock at the age of ten—and reversing and distorting various circumstances within and beyond it, I could depict the background and backstory without having to explain it in tedious alt-historical detail.

The narrator's father is a doctor, not a minister. As a teenager, young Matheson falls under the influence of an orthodox but militant Communism, not Trotskyism. And so on. Some of it is real: Lewis, the RAF base at Aird, and Greenock in the 1960s, are not that different in their texture from my own recollections. Yes, the air pollution really was that bad. Yes, the English voices on Radio Moscow really did sound posh. The 1963 eulogy to Stalin is lifted more or less straight from the real 1953 obituary by Palme Dutt.

The world that Matheson sees is a distorted reflection of the world that his equivalents in our world saw in imagination: one in which the Soviet Union no longer existed as a socialist state, and in which every struggle was part of the apocalyptic confrontation of U.S. imperialism and its allies versus the revolutionary peoples rallied behind the Chinese banner. This view was deluded, as events soon showed, but it resonated even with many who rejected it, including me.

As a schoolboy I was intrigued, to be sure. I studied with some scepticism a copy of the Little Red Book given to me by a Maoist classmate. But by 1972, when I read Han Suyin's rose-tinted rubbish Penguin tract *China in the Year 2001*, I had encountered the theory of state capitalism, which seemed entirely applicable to what was then going on in China—and all the more so to China in the year 2001, as it turned out.

In 1976 I heard on the radio that Mao had died. To my immediate and immense chagrin, I caught myself thinking: *We're on our own now.*

Where, I asked myself, had *that* come from? Writing this story was for me part of finding an answer.

THE FUTURE WILL HAPPEN HERE, TOO

MIAVAIG, IN UIG, ON Lewis, is a scatter of houses—and three churches—across a convergence of hillsides around the place where a short burn connects a loch with a sea-loch. In the culvert where the burn passes under the road lives a black eel that was a good eighteen inches long when I first saw it. (And when it saw me—I remember the cold thrill, a new experience then, when its eyes looked back.) It or its replacement—the wee burn, a hundred yards long and a few inches deep, was wriggling with elvers—may be longer now. I don't know. I've never been back to look, except in dreams.

Around Uig you can find deep, dark glens and wide sandy beaches. There are traces everywhere of a more populous past: the old drove roads snaking across the hills, the roofless rectangles of black houses, the drystone walls under green mounds of moss and turf. It's like growing up in a single enormous ruin that compasses all you see, and includes, in a child's imagination, the rusting carcasses of cars and buses on the moors, the pools of a tidal fish-trap locally attributed to the Vikings, and the brochs and standing stones far away. Above it all were installations of a present guarding against a possible future: the radio mast on a hilltop, the big radar dish revolving black against the sky at the headland of Aird, overlooking the angular concrete blocks of the RAF base.

I lived in Miavaig until I was ten, and then we moved to Greenock, on the Clyde. For summer holidays we always went to Lochcarron, in Wester Ross. The contrast between Uig and Lochcarron was, to me at the time, stark. Lochcarron had far more, and far taller and more various, trees. Some hillsides around it were forested (in Miavaig, a stand of a few spindly pines was called "the plantation"). Its gardens were lush and sprouted exotica—clumps of pampas grass, endless rhododendrons, monkey-puzzle trees. Fires burned wood and coal, not peat. Most people spoke English in everyday life. The hills were higher and the loch was wide and deep.

Across that loch and to the west lay Plockton, a village on a sheltered shore, whose surroundings were lusher even than Lochcarron's: calm waters, green glens and slopes, numerous islets bearing stands of Scots pine, the whole aspect a sight-line for red-and-black sunsets whenever the rain isn't marching in from the west. A short drive south, and up, and you're on the bleak rocky moors of Duirinish and Balmacara, the shadows purple with heather in the late summer.

On these landscapes of early memory I've inflicted science fiction. Made them the battlefields of wars both guerrilla and global. Crashed flying saucers and tactical nukes into them. Crushed them under the mechanical sprawl of runaway artificial intelligences. Choked them with mutant jungles. Made their sea-lochs ring with the din of spaceship yards. Settled their villages with ageless retirees scoffing illegal life-extension drugs. Carpeted their roofs and walls with thick insulation against the big freeze as the Gulf Stream downshifts. And, on the plus side, expanded their villages into thriving industrial towns, repopulating the glens as the Brahan Seer foretold. I've even let the *Press and Journal* soldier on, through wars and revolutions and across the collapse and rebuilding of civilization, into a future several centuries hence.

I haven't spared the urban landscapes I've lived in either. Turned Greenock into a vast naval base, Edinburgh into a dark haunt of terrorists and robots, Waverley Station into the target of a cruise missile strike, Glasgow into a civil war zone, the Clyde into a string of crater lochs, the Firth of Forth into a frontier in a fragmented Britain, and both of the Forth's great bridges into mangled wreckage. But again on the plus side, I've also imagined these cities enduring, Edinburgh reinvent itself as a biotechnology capital, West Lothian flourish as Carbon Glen, and the University of Glasgow sail on through dark centuries as an ark of reason, which one of the characters hails as the Church of Man.

In *Sin Bio*, [eventually *Intrusion*, Orbit, 2012] the novel I'm writing at the moment, I again revisit Lewis—and indeed Miavaig, though not under that name. All I've done to it so far is marred its every horizon with windfarms, and opened what may be a time portal under a hill, but I plot a lot more harm to the place as the book goes on.

This talk about damage is, of course, a joke. You can't really hurt a place by using it as a setting for fiction, no matter how dark the tale. Quite the contrary. The real life of a place is added to if it's lived in imagination, including in the imaginations of people who've never been there. This seems plain enough for mainstream fiction—Greenock has never looked finer than it does in *A Green Tree in Gedde*, and Edinburgh's sense of itself (never knowingly undersold, as the John Lewis advertising boast goes) has gained even in tourism revenue from its many grim phantoms from Deacon Brodie to DI Rebus—but science fiction can add an extra shiver of significance by saying of a place: the future will happen here, too. In an age of increasingly metropolitan media focus, it's easy to accept that Paris, London, New York and all the other cities so readily evoked by their recognisable skylines in disaster movies and in technothrillers should have their place in imagined futures. But other towns and villages and open spaces will still be there, and deserve their piece of the action as part of our futures. Even futures that didn't happen. Without the Martians, who would have heard of Woking? Today, maybe in grateful civic recognition of this, Wells's alien invaders are memorialised by a fine steel statue of a Fighting Machine looming over the pedestrian precinct in the town centre.

So . . . no apologies to the city fathers, the toon cooncillors, or even the inhabitants of the places in which I've imagined terrible things. Better to be the scene of [imagined] catastrophes than the scene of nothing but what's real or what could well be—a pedestrian precinct indeed. I've imagined happy events there too, love and sex, great deeds accomplished, enlightenments gained. The sense of presence in absence, like the ringing of the ears in silence, that I felt as a boy on hot, quiet afternoons climbing the side of Glen Valtos or clambering around the pools and boulders of the gully of the Alt-na-chuirn has echoed in the brains of characters, on this and other planets, who variously interpret it as the mindless mass telepathy of bacteria or the terrible love of God.

Beyond the literal landscapes are their analogues on other worlds. This has to be handled with care, to avoid lazy default to the familiar. For other planets, no matter how Earth-like, I reach for the holiday notebooks and photos and the geology textbooks and the coffee-table travelogues, looking for landforms of karst and fjord, desert and scabland and rainforest, and other features not found to any great extent around here. But sometimes, and consciously, I've reproduced Scotland even there, with variations: a moorland with a henge on every surrounding hilltop, a port town where the haar rolls in every day, a garden where bat-winged aliens get drunk on the alcohol from overripe fruit. (Maybe that last is too obviously the Pear Tree in Edinburgh.)

Behind all these arguable reasons—the kind of recognition and respect such re-creations imply, the realism gained by making use of places I know well enough to depict in detail—there's something more personal. Mostly it's love of the places (mostly—I once took a small but sweet revenge on Dornie for what years in it did to a couple of my friends). But it's also an acknowledgement that Scotland's streets and mountains, lochs and rain have shaped my own mind just as geological processes have carved the landscape itself. This land I live in is still the place I visit in dreams. I owe it that forming, that weathering, that uplift.

"WORKING THE WET END"
KEN MACLEOD INTERVIEWED BY TERRY BISSON

Did you steal the idea for talking squids in outer space from Margaret Atwood? Or from the squids themselves?

As far as I know the only SF writers who have talking squids in outer space are Steve Baxter and myself. I like telling people that I'm responsible for fifty percent of what Margaret Atwood insists she doesn't write.

The idea came out of a pub lunch with Iain Banks in 1980. We started wondering how much of the UFO mythos we could crowbar into a story that made some kind of sense. The Greys were easy: they're so humanoid they are (in our view at the time, anyway) unlikely to have evolved anywhere but Earth, and they're reptilian, so we figured they were probably derived from bipedal dinosaurs. Since there's no trace of humanoid dinosaurs in the fossil record, they must have been taken *off* Earth, which gets us an uplift scenario. That was where the squids came in: the only invertebrates that show potential for intelligence are the cephalopods, so squids were a good candidate for uplift too. And that gave us an explanation of the cigar-shaped motherships, which were so common in the early 1950s and are now so sadly rare: they have to be that size to make room for the aquaria for giant squids to live in. And they have flashing lights on the outside because cephalopods communicate by changing the colour patterns on their skin.

See? It all makes sense!

You are an actual working scientist. Is that what drew you to SF, or did it happen the other way?

I'm not an actual working scientist. Here's the real story: It was SF that drew me to science, or at any rate made me want to be a scientist. Because I was no good at math, I chose the least mathematical science, biology, and specialised in zoology, and within that in vertebrate zoology. This was such a useless specialty that I was the only one in my class who took it.

In choosing my postgraduate work, I made the mistake of thinking I could at least make use of my high-school applied mechanics, and chose a project on the response of bones to mechanical loading. After a year and a half of my slow and intermittent research progress, my supervisors said they couldn't justify my funding. But they kindly continued to supervise my research, which I struggled on with in my spare time for years, and eventually got an M.Phil. degree and my name on a published paper out of. By this time I had a job as a programmer, and my wife and two young children were in my graduation photo.

One of your characters (Elizabeth, in the Engines of Light *trilogy) asserts, "It is possible to learn from the past." You don't really believe that, do you?*

Of course I do. "History is the trade secret of science fiction"—that quote's attributed to me, but I think I got it from Asimov. History is also the trade secret of politics. Successful politicians left and right read lots of it and learn from it. Heck, just reading Macaulay's *History of England* is a political education, and not just for those who share Macaulay's politics: it's centrally about a revolution, after all.

In your work, intelligence is widespread in the universe, but it's mostly not biological. Huh? Aren't you a biologist?

Well, not quite, as I've explained; and in fact the widespread intelligences in the *Engines of Light* books *are* biological. They're dominant because they actively prevent non-biological intelligence from coming into existence. That's the only way you could have such a scenario, because non-biological intelligence is so obviously better adapted to space.

Think about it. Which is likely to happen faster: the evolution by natural selection of a species with superhuman intelligence, or the development of machines that can think faster than us? My bet would be on the machines. Even if you bring in genetic engineering, all that gets you is a given higher level of intelligence, which you can only improve by further genetic engineering. With artificial intelligence, you can in principle get improved performance just by increasing the clock speed or adding hardware, and beyond that you can upgrade the software or make it self-upgrading. That raises the prospect of runaway intelligence increase, which leaves biological mechanisms and reproduction in the dust.

This is of course Vernor Vinge's Singularity thesis, which—if human-equivalent AI is possible at all, and perhaps even if it's not—has an awful logic to it.

Flying saucers: do they come from Outer Space or Genre History?

Disc-shaped flying machines, and spindly humanoids with big bald heads, were imagined and illustrated in SF magazines in the 1930s, so in that sense they do come from genre history. The story that started the modern flying saucer craze, Kenneth Arnold's 1947 sighting, was of more or less wing-shaped flying objects, which he described as moving like saucers skipped across water. Somehow that got garbled to "flying saucers," perhaps because of the images from the pulps, and the hare was off and running. The whole mythos that has evolved since then is a mixture of misidentification, disinformation, urban legend, rumour, lies, hoaxes, honest mistakes, and so on, and it has interacted with SF all along. It would be interesting to trace these interactions and the mutual feedback between SF and UFO reports.

But having said that, the image of a silvery disc levitating above the landscape is immensely resonant, like the dreams we have of flying, and I suspect this is what gives the UFO mythos its power to fascinate.

Banks, Burns, Doctorow, Clarke, Stevenson (R.L. not Neal),
Robson, Robinson: each in a sentence please.

Iain Banks is my oldest friend, and one of the very few
writers who can do both SF and literary fiction equally
well, or indeed at all. Rabbie Burns is an eruption of free-
thinking, folk tradition, love, sex, and sheer poetry against
a Kirk that tried to smother them all under a wet blan-
ket of guilt. Cory Doctorow is a professional agitator who
writes science fiction in his copious spare time (at least
twenty minutes a day), and a dangerous man who should
be watched. Arthur C. Clarke is unfashionable and under-
rated today but some of his work will be read hundreds of
years from now, and he was second only to Asimov among
the few public intellectuals SF has produced. Robert Louis
Stevenson wrote (among many other things) adventure
stories of great psychological subtlety and insight. Justina
Robson is a friend, so I can't be objective, but I find her
a writer of astonishing range, power, and variety. Kim
Stanley Robinson—well, there's the objectivity problem
again—is one of the most serious SF writers, in the sense
that he really means it: he isn't just playing with cool ideas
but putting something on the line.

What is lablit? What does it mean to "work the wet end" of
something?

Lablit is fiction about scientists—not necessarily or even
usually science fiction, but fiction that has scientists as
central characters and shows realistically what scientific
work is like. I don't know where I got "work the wet end"

from, but I meant practical lab or medical work as op-
posed to administration. I guess it could be applied to literature as well.

Publishing being the dry end?

You said that, not me.

Would you describe Night Sessions *as a police procedural or
an ecclesiastical thriller?*

Both. It's a police procedural set in a possible future in
which religion has been officially marginalised, and religious terrorism suddenly pops up from an unexpected
quarter. But perhaps not so unexpected if you know your
Scottish ecclesiastical history!

How come so many UK leftists are Trots?

Short answer: because Trotskyists in Britain moved fast on
the CP's crisis in the 1950s, and moved with the times in
the 1960s.

  Long answer: in the 1960s in a lot of countries semi-
mass currents arose to the left of the official Communist
Parties. In some countries, including the United States
and West Germany, most of the radicals who wanted to
be revolutionaries became some kind of Maoists. In others, including the UK and France, much the same kind of
people became Trotskyists. I think part of the explanation
goes back to the 1950s, and especially the aftermath of
1956 and the Soviet intervention in Hungary.

The crisis of the Communist Party of Great Britain gave rise to a very serious opposition around a magazine called *The New Reasoner*, involving academics and people with real labour movement roots, which became what's now called the Old New Left. Some of these people were very open to Trotsky's arguments, and none of them were interested in adopting a new personality cult or clinging to the old one.

The funny thing is that in the United States the Trotskyists were much better organised than in Britain. For one thing, they were all in one party, the Socialist Workers Party (except for the Shachtmanites, who were busy becoming social democrats). In Britain they were all in one party too, but it was the Labour Party, and they were split into (at least) three mutually hostile groups. But the largest group was able to intervene in the crisis of the CP and rip off a couple of hundred serious people: intellectuals and trade unionists. Then they picked up more young people from the first wave of anti-nuclear activism—the Aldermaston marches and all that. They proceeded to lose or burn out the best of them, largely because their leader, Gerry Healy, was a thug as well as an ultra-left. The regime in Healy's group was far worse than anything anyone had experienced in the CPGB. Say what you like about Harry Pollitt (the CP's general secretary until 1956) he never thumped another communist, or threw anyone down the stairs. But other Trot groups were there to pick up people from the heap at the bottom of Healy's stairwell. What's worrying, actually, is how many went back up the stairs.

In the United States, the SWP fumbled the CPUSA's crisis, saw the CP left wing walk past them and into the increasingly ultra-left Progressive Labor, and followed up by failing to dive into the Civil Rights struggle. The mass movement they did dive into was the Vietnam anti-war movement, and even there they found themselves to the right of the young radicals who wanted to wave Vietcong flags. They came across as a very staid, conservative organization, rather like the CPUSA itself, and missed the 1960s. It took some doing at the time for a revolutionary organization to recruit almost no one out of SDS, but the SWP managed it.

Two of the British Trotskyist groups of the 1960s, the International Socialists and the International Marxist Group, were very much more open to the so-called counterculture. They didn't frown on kids with long hair who smoked dope. They waved their own Vietcong flags. They shifted farther and faster than the U.S. SWP did on gay liberation, as it was then called. They had plenty of militant working-class struggles to pitch into, which the SWP didn't to the same extent (and it missed out on the ones it did have).

So Britain is infested with ex-Trots instead of with ex-Maoists, which is a small mercy.

What kind of car do you drive? (I ask this of everyone.)

A Mazda 2. I abandoned my Bentley when it ran out of peat.

Old-school tools like socket wrenches and WD40 show up in your Futures. Is this a shameless nod to the Steampunk crowd?

No. I don't know enough about Steampunk as a genre, and what I do know doesn't attract me much. If people want to dress up as Victorians, that's fine by me, but as a genre it seems backward-looking—indeed, that's its whole point. We can do better than that.

What is Semana Negra and why is it important?

Semana Negra in Gijón, Asturias, is an annual literary festival with a crowded and raucous funfair attached, complete with Ferris wheel. Its focus is on crime fiction, or "black novels" as they're called in Spain, with a periphery of attention to comics, westerns, horror, fantasy and science fiction. Hundreds of thousands go to the funfair, and thousands go to the book and film festival off in a corner of it.

Partly because crime writers in the Spanish state and in the wider Spanish-speaking world tend to be left-wing, the event has become part of the class struggle in the region. This July, my wife and I rode from Madrid to Gijón on *el Tren Negro*—the Black Train, which they hire every year to transport dozens of writers and journalists to the festival. We stopped in Mieres, a coal-mining town in the mountains of Asturias, where we were greeted by the mayor and a delegation of striking miners and taken on procession through the town for lunch. The train was delayed because striking miners in the adjacent province had blocked the track; it was a very bitter and militant strike. When we arrived at Gijón a brass band at the station played the "Internationale" as we climbed on the bus. You could get used to this sort of thing!

What is a Big Bad Book? Do you intend to write one someday?

Big and Bad are two separate ambitions. I intend to write at least one and hopefully more big books. One is a space opera that uses as many Golden Age tropes—telepathy, FTL, nearby aliens, sunken continents—as I can rationalise by setting it in the deep future of the universe. My mental working title for it is *Star Princesses of the Lost Galaxy*. The other is a long novel, *Dark Queen's Day*, an exercise in dark lord revisionism set after the next Ice Age. I've been tinkering with plans for that, off and on, for years.

The Bad Book idea comes out of a hankering to write a nonfiction bestseller that's not terribly rigorous intellectually—a high standard, but one I believe I could strive for, frankly. I'm thinking along the lines of a mashup of *Chariots of the Gods?* and *The Shock Doctrine*. This is in lieu of a pension plan, you understand, so I have abandoned all scruples and I'm wide open to suggestions.

You sometimes call yourself a Libertarian. Does that mean you take long drives with Ron Paul in his Oldsmobile?

Yeah, me and the Doc, we're like *that*—no. I respect his anti-war stand, but that's all. And I don't call myself a Libertarian, in the sense of a supporter of the Libertarian Party or anything like that. My usual handwave for my position is "hard-left libertarian" but in practice I just vote Labour.

Steve Jobs once told me that Glasgow was the Silicon Valley of the eighteenth century. What's it like today?

Postindustrial, reinventing itself as a tourist attraction, intellectual hub, and shopping centre, with a lot of poverty and long-term unemployment alongside some real development. Silicon Glen with Clearances.

Like many writers (like myself) you moved mothlike from the provinces to the capital. What was that like for you?

The capital, London, was stimulating but overwhelming. I brought to it a stupid provincial left-wing chauvinism about how much more radical the Scots were, and really underestimated how in outer West London I was living in an area with a socialist and trade union history and—in the 1970s—continuing strength that we can only look back on now with amazement. I met my wife there, though funnily enough she grew up not far from me and knew lots of people I knew. Our children's early years were in Finsbury Park, which wasn't a bad place for kids to encounter the world.

Then way back in 1989 my wife and I got a hankering to move back to Scotland.

A bheil Gàidhlig agaibh?

No, sadly. My parents were both native speakers but they didn't speak Gaelic in the home, in a more or less conscious decision to have us grow up speaking English.

In a book like The Star Fraction *(or* Cosmonaut Keep*), are you planting a row of novels, or do they reseed themselves. How far ahead do you plan?*

With *The Star Fraction* I didn't even plan the book when I started it, let alone have sequels in mind. *Cosmonaut Keep*, however, was definitely planned from the beginning as the start of a series. I didn't plan for it to end up as a trilogy, but by the time I started *Engine City* I was losing my own suspension of disbelief, and decided to wrap it up as decisively and entertainingly as I could.

Are there any other serious writers in Edinburgh besides you and Rowling?

Some few. There's Iain Banks, Charlie Stross, Andrew J. Wilson and Hannu Rajaniemi just in SF, and Ian Rankin, Ron Binns, Regi Claire, Andrew Greig, Lesley Glaister, Brian McCabe, just to name some mainstream novelists and poets in my own circle of friends (and I've probably missed someone and will be dead embarrassed if he or she reads this and notices). Edinburgh's hooching with serious writers, and there are more coming up.

I love the title of your blog, The Early Days of a Better Nation. *What does it mean?*

It comes from Alasdair Gray's motto, "Work as if you lived in the early days of a better nation." It means what it says!

Favorite single malt? (This is for Stan Robinson)

Jura 16 Year Old is my current favourite, and Highland Park and Talisker are both very acceptable.

Who is Hans Moravec? Is he important and why?

Hans Moravec is a roboticist and AI guru who predicted in 2009 that "By 2010 we will see mobile robots as big as people but with cognitive abilities similar in many respects to those of a lizard. The machines will be capable of carrying out simple chores, such as vacuuming, dusting, delivering packages and taking out the garbage" (http://www.scientificamerican.com/article.cfm?id=rise-of-the-robots).

To which I say: "What?" I mean, has this guy ever *seen* a lizard? But to me Moravec is important because he mapped out the path from robots to the Singularity and then to the Simulation Hypothesis, which is basically that the Singularity has already happened and we're living in a virtual reality created by our ancestors' creations. I plundered that whole line of argument for the Fall Revolution books and for *The Restoration Game*. I don't believe it for a second.

What is the most interesting difference between SF in the USA and in the UK? The least?

The most interesting difference is in the origins of each tradition's acquaintance with evolution, and how that has affected everything since. In Britain, we had H.G. Wells, who learned his evolutionary biology directly from Thomas Huxley. In the United States, I don't know who the equivalent of Wells was, but whoever it was seems to have picked evolution up from some Social Darwinist like William Graham Sumner. This is like the difference between getting the gospel from Saint Paul and getting it from Norman Vincent Peale. To this day, British SF writers see evolution as a vast pitiless process that will eventually doom humanity, and U.S. SF writers tend to see it as a chirpy homily to self-reliance. "Think of it as evolution in action."—Well, actually, they don't!

The least interesting difference, in my judgment, is spelling.

You recently took a position teaching writing. Is that a promotion?

I'm not exactly teaching writing—that's what the course tutors do. As Writer in Residence for the M.A. creative writing course at Edinburgh Napier University, my job is to advise the students about writing and just be there to talk to. I'm not even expected to read their work! I definitely see it as a promotion, and I love doing it.

In your works you seem not so much constructing as punching your way out of an already incredibly rich and detailed future. True or false?

False, I'm afraid. I have to construct my detailed futures quite painfully, though nothing like as painfully as I construct my plots and even storylines. World-building is easy; stories are hard.

What's next?

A novel provisionally titled *Descent*, which is at the moment in that very stage of painful construction that I've just mentioned. As usual I've planned it, made lots of notes, got excited, plunged into writing it, got about thirteen thousand words in and found I hadn't planned it enough. I always tell myself I won't do this again, and every time, I do.

What U.S. writer would you most like to have a drink with, besides me?

Howard Waldrop.

I know that Dr. Johnson made it to the Hebrides, with the assistance of Boswell and a donkey. Did he get as far as Stornoway?

Was that Roswell or Boswell? I guess the donkey's a clue. I haven't read the book, but I have it somewhere and I intend to at least skim it.

Ever collaborate?

No. Except on the occasional interview.

Your books are often, and quite correctly, praised for their humor. Say something funny.

I have Ostalgia for the Free World.

BIBLIOGRAPHY

Novels:

The Star Fraction (London: Legend, 1995).
    Arthur C. Clarke Award shortlist; Prometheus
    Award winner
The Stone Canal (London: Legend, 1996).
    Prometheus Award winner
The Cassini Division (London: Orbit, 1998).
    Waterstone's Scottish Book of the Month, May
    1998; Nebula Award shortlist 2000
The Sky Road (London: Orbit, 1999).
    British Science Fiction Association Award winner;
    Hugo Award shortlist 2001
Cosmonaut Keep (London: Orbit, 2000).
    Hugo Award shortlist 2002
Dark Light (London: Orbit, 2001).
    Tiptree Award shortlist 2001; Prometheus Award
    finalist
Engine City (London: Orbit, 2002).

Newton's Wake (London: Orbit, 2004).

> Japanese translation, Seuin Award 2006

Learning the World (London: Orbit, 2005).

> Arthur C. Clarke Award shortlist, 2006;
> Prometheus Award winner

The Execution Channel (London: Orbit, 2007).

> Quills shortlist, 2007; Arthur C. Clarke Award
> shortlist, 2008; Prometheus Award shortlist, 2008;
> John W. Campbell Memorial Award shortlist, 2008

The Night Sessions (London: Orbit, 2008).

> British Science Fiction Association Award winner

The Restoration Game (London: Orbit, 2010).

Intrusion (London: Orbit, 2012).

Novellas:

THE WEB: Cydonia (London: Orion, 1998).

The Human Front (Harrogate: PS Publishing, 2001;

> London: Gollancz 2003).
> Reprinted in *The Year's Best Science Fiction:*
> *Nineteenth Annual Collection*, edited by Gardner
> Dozois (New York: St. Martin's Griffin, 2002).
> Sidewise Award winner

The Highway Men (Dingwall: Sandstone Vistas, 2006).

> Reprinted in *The Year's Best Science Fiction: Twenty-*
> *Fourth Annual Collection*, edited by Gardner
> Dozois (New York: St. Martin's Griffin, 2007).

Short stories:

"Moonlighting," *Sunday Times*, 1998.

"Resident Alien," *Computer Weekly* supplement
  IT@2000, November 1999.
"The Oort Crowd," *Nature* 406, no. 6792, July 13, 2000.
  Reprinted in *The Year's Best SF 6*, edited by David G.
  Hartwell (New York: EOS/HarperCollins, 2001).
"Undead Again," *Nature* 433, no. 7027, February 17, 2005.
  Reprinted in *Futures from Nature*, edited by Henry
  Gee (New York: Tor, 2007).
"Facing the New Atlantic," in *Scotland 2020: hopeful
  stories for a northern nation* (London: Demos 2005).
"A Case of Consilience," in *Nova Scotia: New Scottish
  Speculative Fiction*, eds. Neil Williamson and
  Andrew J. Wilson (Edinburgh: Crescent Books/
  Mercat Press, 2005).
  Reprinted in *The Year's Best Science Fiction: Twenty-Third
  Annual Collection*, edited by Gardner Dozois (New
  York: St. Martin's Griffin, 2006); and in *The Year's
  Best SF 11*, edited by David G. Hartwell and Kathryn
  Kramer (New York: EOS/HarperCollins, 2006).
"Who's Afraid of Wolf 359?" in *The New Space Opera*,
  edited by Gardner Dozois and Jonathan Strahan,
  Harvester, 2006 (Hugo Award shortlist, 2008;
  Locus Award shortlist, 2008)
"Jesus Christ, Reanimator," in Fast Forward 1, edited by
  Lou Anders (Amherst, NY: Pyr, 2007).
  Reprinted in *The Best Science Fiction and Fantasy
  of the Year: Vol. 2*, edited by Jonathan Strahan (San
  Francisco: Night Shade Books, 2008).
"MS Found on a Hard Drive." In *Glorifying Terrorism*,
  edited by Farah Mendlesohn (London: Rackstraw
  Press, 2006).

"Lighting Out," in *disLOCATIONS*, edited by Ian Whates (Alconbury Weston: NewCon Press, 2007). Reprinted in *The Year's Best Science Fiction: Twenty-Fifth Annual Collection*, edited by Gardner Dozois (New York: St. Martin's Griffin, 2008). BSFA Award winner

"Wilson at Woking," in *Celebration*, edited by Ian Whates (Alconbury Weston: NewCon Press, 2008).

"A Dance Called Armageddon," in *Seeds of Change*, edited by John Joseph Adams (Holicong, PA: Prime Books, 2008).

"iThink, Therefore I Am," in *The Solaris Book of New Science Fiction, Volume Three*, edited by George Mann (Nottingham: Solaris Books, 2009).

"Death Knocks," in *When It Changed: Science into Fiction*, edited by Geoff Ryman (Manchester: Comma Press, 2009).

"A Tulip for Lucretius," *Subterranean*, Spring 2009.

"Reflective Surfaces," in *New Scientist* 2726, September 19, 2009.

"Sidewinders," in *The Mammoth Book of Alternate Histories*, edited by Ian Watson and Ian Whates (London: Robinson Publishing, 2010).

"The Vorkuta Event," in *The New and Perfect Man: Postscripts #24/25*, edited by Peter Crowther and Nick Gevers (Hornsea: PS Publishing, 2011).

"Earth Hour," a Tor.com Original (London: Macmillan, 2011).

"The Best Science Fiction of the Year Three," in *Solaris Rising: The New Solaris Book of Science Fiction*, edited by Ian Whates (Oxford: Solaris, 2011).

"The Surface of Last Scattering," in *TRSF*, edited by Stephen Cass (Boston: Technology Review, Inc., 2011).

Nonfiction:

"The Aleppo Button" (review) *New Dawn Fades* 10. "Balkaniziranje Britanije i druge lose zamisli" [Balkanizing Britain and Other Bad Ideas] *Ni riba ni meso*, Zagreb 1, Spring 1996.

"The Encyclopaedia of Fantasy" (review) *Scottish Book Collector* 5, no. 7, Summer 1997.

"The Encyclopaedia of Fantasy" (review) *Free Life* 27, September 1997.

"Libertarianism, the Loony Left and the Secrets of the Illuminati" *Matrix* 127, September–October 1997. Reprinted as *Personal Perspectives* 10, Libertarian Alliance, 1998.

"Science Fiction After the Future Went Away," *revolution* 5, March 1998.

"SF: No Future in It?" *LM* 116, December 1998/January 1999.

"History in SF: What (Hasn't Yet) Happened in History," In *Histories of the Future: Studies in Fact, Fantasy and Science Fiction*, edited by Alan Sandison and Robert Dingley (New York: Palgrave, 2000).

"Rewriting Humanity: Reflections on the Possibility and Desirability of Genetic Engineering," *Scientific Notes* 13, Libertarian Alliance, 2001.

"Whole Wide World" (review), *Foundation: The International Review of Science Fiction* 31, no. 84, Spring 2002.

"Singularity Skies," *Locus* 51, no. 2 (issue no. 511) (August 2003): 41–42.

"Politics and Science Fiction." In *The Cambridge Companion to Science Fiction*, edited by Edward James and Farah Mendlesohn (Cambridge: Cambridge University Press, 2003).

"Space." *Sunday Herald*, March 2004.

"Socialism on One Planet." *Socialist Standard*, June 2004.

"Does SF Have to Be About the Present?" *New York Review of Science Fiction*, Fall 2004.

"I Robot, You Robot?" *BT Business Together*, 2004.

"Islands, Funerals, and the Footnotes of Buckle." *The Scorpion 2*, 2005.

"The Profession of Science Fiction: Seeing Through the Atmosphere," *Foundation: The International Review of Science Fiction* 36, no. 99, Spring 2007.

"The Biologists Strike Back," (contributor) *Nature* 448 (July 5, 2007): 18–21.

"Refloating the Ark," *Morning Star*, March 3, 2008.

"*Blood Music*, Greg Bear, 1985," *SFX*, July 2008.

"*A Case of Conscience*, James Blish, 1958," *SFX*, December 2008.

"*Flood*, by Stephen Baxter" (review), *Foundation: The International Review of Science Fiction* 38, no. 105, Spring 2009.

"*The Centauri Device*, M. John Harrison, 1974," *SFX*, October 2009.

"Space Odyssey," with Dr. Duncan Steel, *BBC Focus Magazine* 198, January 2009.

"Reading the Genome," *ESRC Genomics Network Newsletter* 9, Spring 2009.

"*Starship Troopers*, Robert A. Heinlein, 1959," *SFX*, February 2010.

"Humanity Will Thank Heaven That This Creator of Synthetic Life Is Playing God," *Guardian*, May 21, 2010.

"Gattaca," in *Cinema Futura*, edited by Mark Morris, PS Publishing, 2010.

"*Cities in Flight*, James Blish, 1970," *SFX*, November 2010.

"Engaging the Public with Genomics through Literary Networks and Fan Communities," Genomics Forum Briefing, edited by Dr. Christine Knight, 2010.

"Living with the Genome—Ten Years On," with Dr. Steve Sturdy, *The Gen*, September 2010.

"The Future Will Happen Here, Too," in *The Bottle Imp* 8, Fall 2010, Association for Scottish Literary Studies.

"Science Fiction Opens Up the Universe," *Guardian*, July 14, 2011.

Collection (fiction, nonfiction, and poems):

Giant Lizards from Another Star, NESFA Press, 2006.

Poems:

"Faith as a Grain of Poppy Seed," *Poetry and Audience* 23, no. 3.

"Succession," *New Dawn Fades* 10.

Poems and Polemics (Minneapolis: Rune Press, 2001).

Editorial responsibilities:

The Human Genre Project, a website of poetry and short
   prose pieces (stories and reflections) inspired by
   genetics and genomics. The website is supported
   by the ESRC Genomics Policy and Research
   Forum.
   http://www.humangenreproject.com/index.php.

Critical discussions:

The True Knowledge of Ken MacLeod, edited by Andrew
   M. Butler and Farah Mendlesohn (Reading: The
   Science Fiction Foundation, 2003).
"'What's Past Is Prologue': Historical Causation and
   Agency in Ken MacLeod's *The Star Fraction* and
   The Stone Canal," John H. Arnold, *Foundation: The
   International Review of Science Fiction* 34, no. 93,
   Spring 2005.
"Ken MacLeod and the Practice of History," Sherryl
   Vint, *Foundation: The International Review of
   Science Fiction* 35, no. 96, Spring 2006.
"Ken MacLeod's Permanent Revolution: Utopian
   Possible Worlds, History, and the *Augenblick* in the
   'Fall Revolution,'" Philip Wegner, in *Red Planets:
   Marxism and Science Fiction*, edited by Mark
   Bould and China Miéville (London: Pluto Press,
   2009).

ABOUT THE AUTHOR

KEN MACLEOD WAS BORN in Stornoway, Isle of Lewis, Scotland, on August 2, 1954. He is married with two grown-up children and lives in West Lothian. He has honours and master's degree in biological subjects and worked for some years in the IT industry.

Since 1997 he has been a full-time writer. In 2009 he was Writer in Residence at the ESRC Genomics Policy and Research Forum at Edinburgh University, and is now Writer in Residence at the MA Creative Writing course at Edinburgh Napier University.

He is the author of thirteen novels, from *The Star Fraction* (Legend, 1995) to *Intrusion* (Orbit, 2012), and many articles and short stories. His novels and stories have received three BSFA Awards and three Prometheus Awards, and several have been short-listed for the Clarke and Hugo Awards.

Ken MacLeod's blog is *The Early Days of a Better Nation* (http://kenmacleod.blogspot.com). His Twitter feed is @amendlocke.

PM PRESS
OUTSPOKEN AUTHORS

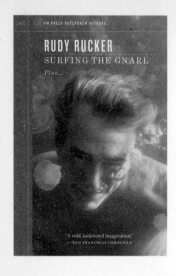

Surfing the Gnarl
Rudy Rucker
128 Pages
$12.00

The original "Mad Professor" of Cyberpunk, Rudy Rucker (along with fellow outlaws William Gibson and Bruce Sterling) transformed modern science fiction, tethering the "gnarly" speculations of quantum physics to the noir sensibilities of a skeptical and disenchanted generation. In acclaimed novels like *Wetware* and *The Hacker and the Ant* he mapped a neotopian future that belongs not to sober scientists but to drug-addled, sex-crazed youth. And won legions of fans doing it.

In his outrageous new *Surfing the Gnarl*, Dr. Rucker infiltrates fundamentalist Virginia to witness the apocalyptic clash between Bible-thumpers and Saucer Demons at a country club barbecue; undresses in orbit to explore the future of foreplay in freefall ("Rapture in Space"); and (best of all!) dons the robe of a Transreal Lifestyle Adviser with How-to Tips on how you can manipulate the Fourth Dimension to master everyday tasks like finding an apartment, dispatching a tiresome lover, organizing closets and iPods, and remaking Reality.

You'll never be the same. Is that good or bad? Your call.

PM PRESS
OUTSPOKEN AUTHORS

Report from Planet Midnight
Nalo Hopkinson
128 Pages
$12.00

Nalo Hopkinson has been busily (and wonderfully) "subverting the genre" since her first novel, *Brown Girl in the Ring*, won a Locus Award for SF and Fantasy in 1999. Since then she has acquired a prestigious World Fantasy Award, a legion of adventurous and aware fans, a reputation for intellect seasoned with humor, and a place of honor in the short list of SF writers who are tearing down the walls of category and transporting readers to previously unimagined planets and realms.

Never one to hold her tongue, Hopkinson takes on sexism and racism in publishing ("Report from Planet Midnight") in a historic and controversial presentation to her colleagues and fans.

Plus...

"Message in a Bottle," a radical new twist on the time travel tale that demolishes the sentimental myth of childhood innocence; and "Shift," a tempestuous erotic adventure in which Caliban gets the girl. Or does he?

And Featuring: our Outspoken Interview, an intimate one-on-one that delivers a wealth of insight, outrage, irreverence, and top-secret Caribbean spells.

"Rapidly emerging as the William Gibson of his generation."
—ENTERTAINMENT WEEKLY

PM PRESS
OUTSPOKEN AUTHORS

The Great Big Beautiful Tomorrow
Cory Doctorow
144 Pages
$12.00

Cory Doctorow burst on the SF scene in 2000 like a rocket, inspiring awe in readers (and envy in other writers) with his bestselling novels and stories, which he insisted on giving away via Creative Commons. Meanwhile, as coeditor of the wildly popular blog Boing Boing, he became the radical new voice of the Web, boldly arguing for internet freedom from corporate control.

Doctorow's activism and artistry are both on display in this Outspoken Author edition. The crown jewel is his novella, "The Great Big Beautiful Tomorrow," the high-velocity adventures of a transhuman teenager in a toxic post-Disney dystopia, battling wireheads and wumpuses (and having fun doing it!) until he meets the "meat girl" of his dreams, and is forced to choose between immortality and sex.

Plus a live transcription of Cory's historic address to the 2010 World SF Convention, "Creativity vs. Copyright," dramatically presenting his controversial case for open-source in both information and art.

Also included is an international Outspoken Interview (skyped from England, Canada, and the U.S.) in which Doctorow reveals the surprising sources of his genius.

FRIENDS OF

These are indisputably momentous times—the financial system is melting down globally and the Empire is stumbling. Now more than ever there is a vital need for radical ideas.

In the six years since its founding—and on a mere shoestring—PM Press has risen to the formidable challenge of publishing and distributing knowledge and entertainment for the struggles ahead. With over 250 releases to date, we have published an impressive and stimulating array of literature, art, music, politics, and culture. Using every available medium, we've succeeded in connecting those hungry for ideas and information to those putting them into practice.

Friends of PM allows you to directly help impact, amplify, and revitalize the discourse and actions of radical writers, filmmakers, and artists. It provides us with a stable foundation from which we can build upon our early successes and provides a much-needed subsidy for the materials that can't necessarily pay their own way. You can help make that happen—and receive every new title automatically delivered to your door once a month—by joining as a Friend of PM Press. And, we'll throw in a free T-Shirt when you sign up.

Here are your options:

- $25 a month: Get all books and pamphlets plus 50% discount on all webstore purchases
- $40 a month: Get all PM Press releases (including CDs and DVDs) plus 50% discount on all webstore purchases
- $100 a month: Superstar—Everything plus PM merchandise, free downloads, and 50% discount on all webstore purchases

For those who can't afford $25 or more a month, we're introducing Sustainer Rates at $15, $10, and $5. Sustainers get a free PM Press t-shirt and a 50% discount on all purchases from our website.

Your Visa or Mastercard will be billed once a month, until you tell us to stop. Or until our efforts succeed in bringing the revolution around. Or the financial meltdown of Capital makes plastic redundant. Whichever comes first.

PM Press was founded at the end of 2007 by a small collection of folks with decades of publishing, media, and organizing experience. PM Press co-conspirators have published and distributed hundreds of books, pamphlets, CDs, and DVDs. Members of PM have founded enduring book fairs, spearheaded victorious tenant organizing campaigns, and worked closely with bookstores, academic conferences, and even rock bands to deliver political and challenging ideas to all walks of life. We're old enough to know what we're doing and young enough to know what's at stake.

We seek to create radical and stimulating fiction and non-fiction books, pamphlets, t-shirts, visual and audio materials to entertain, educate and inspire you. We aim to distribute these through every available channel with every available technology—whether that means you are seeing anarchist classics at our bookfair stalls; reading our latest vegan cookbook at the café; downloading geeky fiction e-books; or digging new music and timely videos from our website.

PM Press is always on the lookout for talented and skilled volunteers, artists, activists and writers to work with. If you have a great idea for a project or can contribute in some way, please get in touch.

PM Press
PO Box 23912
Oakland CA 94623
510-658-3906
www.pmpress.org